For Evan and Holly

Rookie
of the
Year

PhiL BiLDNeR
Roo
of
Ye

By Phil Bildner

The Rip and Red Series

A Whole New Ballgame
Rookie of the Year
Tournament of Champions

The Sluggers Series
with Loren Long

Magic in the Outfield
Horsin' Around
Great Balls of Fire
Water, Water Everywhere
Blastin' the Blues
Home of the Brave

pictures by TIM PROBERT

SQUARE FISH

Farrar Straus Giroux
New York

SQUARE FISH

An imprint of Macmillan Publishing Group, LLC
175 Fifth Avenue
New York, NY 10010
mackids.com

Our books may be purchased in bulk for promotional, educational, or business use.
Please contact your local bookseller or the Macmillan Corporate and Premium
Sales Department at (800) 221-7945 ext. 5442 or by e-mail at
MacmillanSpecialMarkets@macmillan.com.

Library of Congress Cataloging-in-Publication Data
Names: Bildner, Phil. | Probert, Tim, illustrator.
Title: Rookie of the year / Phil Bildner ; pictures by Tim Probert.
Description: New York : Farrar Straus Giroux, 2016. | Series: Rip and Red | Summary: "Rip and Red find that fifth grade continues to challenge them in brand-new ways and discover that sometimes radical change is nothing to be afraid of"—Provided by publisher.
Identifiers: LCCN 2015022215 | ISBN 978-1-250-11518-8 (paperback) | ISBN 978-0-374-30135-4 (ebook)
Subjects: | CYAC: Schools—Fiction. | Best friends—Fiction. | Friendship—Fiction. | Basketball—Fiction. | People with disabilities—Fiction. | BISAC: JUVENILE FICTION / Sports & Recreation / Basketball. | JUVENILE FICTION / Social Issues / Friendship. | JUVENILE FICTION / School & Education.
Classification: LCC PZ7.B4923 Roo 2016 | DDC [Fic]—dc23
LC record available at http://lccn.loc.gov/2015022215

Originally published in the United States by Farrar Straus Giroux
First Square Fish edition: 2017
Book designed by Andrew Arnold
Square Fish logo designed by Filomena Tuosto

3 5 7 9 10 8 6 4 2

AR: 3.9 / LEXILE: 550L

Rookie
of the
Year

Cafeteria Basketball

"It all comes down to this," I said, announcing the play-by-play. "Ten seconds on the clock, Clifton United trails by two. Irving has the ball at the top of the key."

Actually, I was standing on a table in the middle of the empty school cafeteria, and the ball was really the crumpled tinfoil wrappers that had contained the last of my Halloween candy. I sized up the garbage can in front of the LINE STARTS HERE sign on the wall by the food-serving area.

"Hurry up, Mason Irving," Red said.

I'm Mason Irving. That's what Red calls me. Everyone else calls me Rip.

Red was by the entrance on lookout.

He gripped the headphones hooked around his neck with one hand and tapped his leg with the other.

"Irving jab-steps left." I pretended to dribble. "He slides right, looking to create some space."

Red and I were allowed to be in the cafeteria in the morning. We had a pass from our teacher, Mr. Acevedo. But I probably wasn't allowed to be standing on a table playing tinfoil basketball.

Make that *definitely* wasn't allowed.

"Hurry up," Red said again.

Just so you know, I wasn't going to miss this shot. The new basketball season started right after school, and this was my good-luck, half-court-heave, buzzer-beating basket before the first practice.

No way was I going to miss this shot.

"Five seconds . . . four," I counted down. I brushed the dreadlocks off my forehead. "Three . . . two . . . from three-point land!"

I baseball-threw the tinfoil, and with my basketball eyes I tracked its flight over the tables.

It landed in the center of the can.

"Boo-yah!" I hammer-fisted the air.

"Bam!" Red cheered.

The Early Pass

You might be wondering why two fifth graders are allowed to be all by themselves in the cafeteria, so let me explain.

Each morning, I meet Red at the end of his driveway,

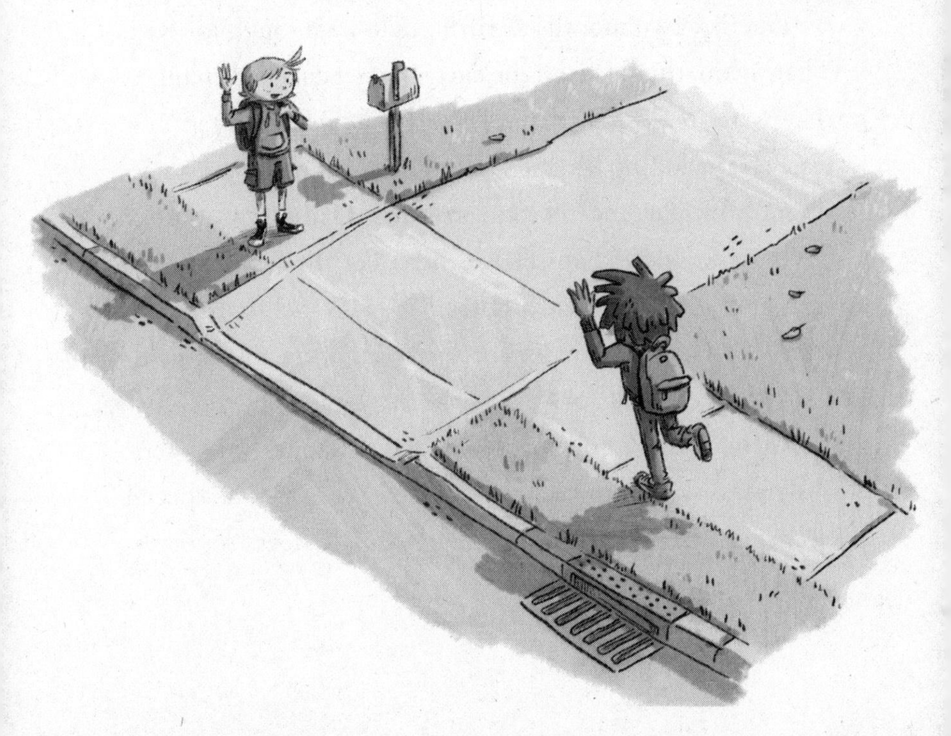

and we walk to Reese Jones Elementary. We cut through the school yard, zigzag through the portables (the second- and third-grade classrooms), and obstacle-course the new playground. We reach the main entrance to RJE just as the building officially opens.

The same thing, every day.

But for the last couple weeks, I've been meeting Red ten minutes earlier because he's now permitted in the building before the other kids. He's allowed to go up to our classroom, get unpacked, and settle in before everyone else. Since I walk to school with Red, I'm allowed in early, too.

Here's why:

The first two months of fifth grade were tough for Red. Then again, thanks to all the crazy budget cuts and changes, they were tough for all the kids. There were like ten new teachers, including Mr. Acevedo. There was no longer an assistant principal, and the principal, Ms. Darling, was out of the building more than she was here. For the first time, the fifth graders had to switch classes. We also had to eat lunch with the first and second graders, instead of the fourth graders. Luckily, we still got to sit in the fifth-grade-only booths.

As for Red, he doesn't do well with changes. They seriously mess with him. That's why Ms. Yvonne—the special ed teacher—suggested the building pass. Red does a lot better when he gets to places early or on time.

The thing is, the early pass only gets us into RJE. It doesn't allow us to roam the halls. That's where Mr. Acevedo comes in. He doesn't mind us leaving Room 208 so long as we're back when the other kids arrive.

It's pretty cool being the only kids in the school and walking past the front doors while everyone else is outside, especially since it's the beginning of November and getting a little cooler. And it's beyond pretty cool playing tinfoil hoops in an empty cafeteria.

The Lunch Bunch

After I sank my long-distance tinfoil shot, we started back to Room 208.

"The new lunch ladies completely ignore us, Mason Irving," Red said.

"They don't even know we're in there," I said.

"Ms. Eunice, Ms. Carmen, Ms. Joan, Ms. Audrey, and Ms. Liz would never completely ignore us like the new lunch ladies. I miss the Lunch Bunch."

I raised my fist. "Bring back the Lunch Bunch!"

The Lunch Bunch. That's what we used to call the lunch ladies. They'd been at RJE since before we started kindergarten. But because of the cuts, they were replaced.

None of the kids like the new cafeteria people. They don't play music during grab-and-go breakfast. They don't sing and dance when they serve lunch. They don't talk to us or know any of our names (except for the kids who act up).

"The Lunch Bunch would never let you stand on the table, Mason Irving."

"Not in a gazillion years."

"Especially Ms. Eunice!"

I laughed. "If Ms. Eunice caught me standing on one of her tables, she'd throw my butt in the trash can!"

Up ahead, Mr. Goldberg, the head custodian, was walking toward the front doors with his keys out. Ms. Waldon, the parent coordinator, was arranging the papers on her desk under the announcement monitor in the main hall.

Mr. Goldberg and Ms. Waldon know everything about RJE. Everything.

"Happy Monday, boys," Ms. Waldon said.

"Hi, Ms. Waldon." Red waved.

"You boys have a nice weekend?"

"Oh, yeah," Red said. "Did you?"

"I did. Thanks for asking."

"You're welcome, Ms. Waldon."

Red and Ms. Waldon have a conversation like this every morning.

We turned down the K–1 hallway and headed for the staircase. The K–1 stairs are the only stairs Red will use at RJE.

"Do you think this basketball season will be the same as last basketball season?" Red asked.

"I guess so," I said.

"Do you think Coach Acevedo will run practices the same way he ran practices last season?"

Our teacher, Mr. Acevedo, is also Coach Acevedo, our basketball coach.

"I guess so," I said again.

We two-at-a-timed the steps, leaped around the cans of paint and rolls of brown paper on the middle landing, and charged onto the second floor.

"Rip and Red!" Xander shouted, racing up.

"Hey, Xander McDonald," Red said.

Xander is in our class. Everyone calls him X, except for Red. Red calls everyone by his or her first and last name.

"I heard you two are the only ones from RJE on Clifton United again," Xander said.

"You heard right," I said.

"Just like last season," Red said.

Clifton United is the name of our basketball team. Until this year, the fifth-grade basketball program was only open to RJE kids, but now it's a district-wide fifth-grade team open to all kids in Clifton.

"Noah wanted to play," I said, "but his family is going on vacation in December. He'd have to miss the last two weeks."

"You think you'll win more than one game this time?" Xander asked.

I shrugged. "Anything's possible."

We walked past the library and headed for Room 208 at the end of the hall. When we reached the door, we stopped dead in our tracks.

A girl was talking with Mr. Acevedo, a girl we'd never seen before.

Takara Eid

"This is Takara," Mr. Acevedo said after everyone had arrived. He stood next to her at the front of the class. "She's joining us in here. Room 208 has a new addition."

A new addition?

The fifth grade never got new students. In the lower grades, kids came and went all the time, and each grade also had three or four classes. But the fifth grade had only one class. The last time we got new kids was when the twins, Lana and Ana, moved here in second grade.

"Would you like to introduce yourself?" Mr. Acevedo asked.

"Yeppers," she said.

A couple kids snickered. Mr. Acevedo silenced them with a stare.

"I'm Takara," she said. She held up her arms and pushed her hip out to the side like a dancer at the end of a number. "Takara Eid. But everyone calls me Tiki. I'm Egyptian. Well, my pop's from Egypt." She patted her cheeks and tilted her head. "That's why I'm brown."

A lot more than a couple kids wanted to snicker—including me. But the don't-you-dare lasers shooting from Mr. Acevedo's eyes stopped us.

Tiki wore a bright yellow hoodie shirt with the Eiffel Tower on the front, purple pants like Trinity's and Attie's, and light-blue canvas low-tops with one white shoelace and one black shoelace.

"So we now have thirteen girls and thirteen boys," Melissa said.

"We do," Mr. Acevedo said.

"We've never had as many girls." She stood up, looked down at Noah sitting next to her, and smiled. "We're bigger than you, too."

The girls were bigger than the boys this year. Whenever I stood next to Melissa, Grace, or Isa, I felt like I was their little brother.

The biggest boy, Bryan, was no longer in the class. He was the biggest kid at RJE. But his family had to move. Mr. Acevedo told us about it last week during CC, Community Circle. That's our class meeting time.

"Let's see where I'm going to put you, Tiki." Mr. Acevedo brushed some hair off his face and looked around the room. "Rip and Red, there are two open seats at your table. I'm going to have her join you."

"Which one of you is Rip?" Tiki blurted loudly.

I started to reply but she cut me off.

"Gollygadzookers." She snort-laughed. She patted her cheeks again. "I can't believe I said that out loud. Of course I know which one of you is Red."

"People call me Red because of my hair," Red said. "My real name is Blake Daniels. Rip's real name is Mason Irving."

She looked right at me. "There was a kid at my old school named Rip." She pumped her eyebrows. "Everyone called him Rip because he ripped farts all the time."

Everyone laughed.

Everyone but me.

"That's not why people call me Rip," I said.

She held up her hands with her fingers spread apart. "Could you imagine if that was the reason? That would be so freakaliciously funny."

My cheeks blazed. Some people don't think black people blush or turn red, but trust me, we do.

I let out a loud puff. This was how nicknames got started. Bad nicknames. Bad nicknames that stuck. Like a fart nickname. A fart nickname the year before middle school.

"So what does . . . what does your name mean?" I asked.

"*Eid* means 'festival'!" She raised her arms again. "So if

your last name was Eid, and you farted a lot, it would be a farting festival!"

Everyone laughed again.

I didn't.

"Rip," Mr. Acevedo said, "take Tiki around today. Show her Room 208. Show her what RJE is all about."

Tiki Time

I stared at Tiki. She sat straight across from me. She and Red were chatting like besties.

"Mr. Acevedo's a big fan of breaks," Red said. "That's why we're taking one now."

"I'm a big fan of breaks, too," Tiki said, smiling.

"Breaks last about five to ten minutes," Red said.

"It would be horrible if cars and trucks didn't stop!" Tiki leaned forward. "I'm a big fan of *brakes*, too."

"Mr. Acevedo is not a big fan of homework." Red kept going. "Mr. Acevedo's not a big fan of tests."

"Something tells me Mr. Acevedo's not a big fan of worksheets either."

"Mr. Acevedo's not, Takara Eid!" Red pointed to the large NWZ—No Worksheet Zone—sign next to the white-board.

I let out a puff.

After Bryan left last week, Mr. Acevedo said everyone

could change seats, but Red and I didn't because we liked our seats by the windows, and Red only sits facing doors. Miles moved to a table in the back so he could sit with Noah, and Trinity moved to the middle table with the OMG girls—Olivia, Mariam, and Grace. That meant the two seats across from Red and me were open. We had the table to ourselves.

Until . . .

"Do you know what T3 is, Takara Eid?" Red asked.

"I have a hunchabalooga you're going to tell me, Blake Daniels."

"*Hunchabalooga* isn't even a word," I said.

"It is to me." Tiki pointed to herself with both index fingers. "I love making up words."

"T3 is Teacher's Theater Time," Red said. "That's when Mr. Acevedo reads to the class. Mr. Acevedo reads to the class every day. Mr. Acevedo's the best reader."

"You can't just make up words," I said.

"Why not?" Tiki placed her elbows on the table and cupped her hands around her chin. "I love having my own words. It's so much fun. Fa-real-zees. That means for real."

"You can't do that."

"Who says?"

I twisted a lock near my forehead at its root and looked over at Mr. Acevedo. He was sitting on the lip of the bathtub in the meeting area, talking with Diego and Xander.

Why do I have to show her around? Why can't somebody else?

"At this one school I went to," Tiki said, "there were fifteen fifth-grade classes. Fifteen! And at this other school, there were only forty-four kids in the whole school."

"How many schools have you been to, Takara Eid?" Red asked.

"This year?" She counted fingers. "Four."

"Why do you move around so much?" I asked.

"We just do," she said.

"We call independent reading Choice," Red said. "We call it Choice because we're allowed to read whatever we want."

"I like reading nonfiction," Tiki said.

"Most of the nonfiction is over there." Red pointed to the corner by the Swag Wall. "Some of the nonfiction is on top of the cubbies in the silver toolboxes. Some of the nonfiction is in the orange, green, and yellow milk crates."

Ms. Yvonne walked in.

"Hi, Ms. Yvonne." Red waved.

"Hi, Red," Ms. Yvonne said, heading for our table. "And you must be Takara."

"Yeppers," she said. "Everyone calls me Tiki, except for Red."

Ms. Yvonne sat down. "Honey, why don't you put those away?" She nodded to the headphones still around Red's neck. "You don't need them now."

Red slipped them off his neck, spun them around his wrist, and rolled them into his desk. Red can do tons of cool tricks with his headphones.

"As soon as break ends," Ms. Yvonne said to Red, "we're going over your writer's notebook."

"Thanks, Ms. Yvonne."

"I want to see yours, too," she said to me.

Whenever Ms. Yvonne was in ELA—which was most of the time—she helped all the kids, not just the ones with services.

I tilted back my chair, grabbed a composition notebook from the windowsill, and slid it across to Tiki.

"Here," I said.

"All your writing work goes in there." Ms. Yvonne tapped the cover. "So you're from Egypt, Tiki?"

"My family is."

"Have you ever been?"

"Not yet." Her thick eyebrows curved up. "Most of my family has. Pop was raised there."

"Pop?" I said. "You call your dad Pop?"

"Yeppers."

I let out a puff and checked the clock. Less than three hours until lunch.

Name That Food

"Ambush!" I reached across the table and jabbed Diego's arm with my spork.

"Spork war!" He swiped at my hand with his.

We were in the cafeteria, sitting at a fifth-grade booth along the side wall.

I half stood, leaned in, and poked at Diego's shoulder. When he jumped back, I tried flicking the strings on his hat. He ducked away, lunged forward, and stabbed the corner of my tray. I went for his fingers, scratching his knuckles.

"Yo!" Diego stood.

"Everyone, stop!" Avery held out her hands and looked at Diego. "Dude, sit down. You friggin' splashed me."

"It was either water . . . It was either water, skim milk, or tropical cranberry juice," Red stammered.

Avery and Red were at the booth, too. Avery was parked at the end. Red was next to me.

I swiped at Diego again. "Ambush!"

"Stop!" Avery spun her wheelchair to me and smacked my hand. "I mean it, dude. Stop."

I stopped. But not because of Avery.

Because of Red.

His fists were next to his eyes. They were trembling. His shoulders were hunched, and his face was squinched.

Red doesn't like play fighting, especially rough play fighting. He doesn't like being touched or hit. He doesn't like getting in trouble either. Not that Red was doing anything wrong or that he ever really got in trouble. But he was next to kids who could get him in trouble. The whole time Diego and I were battling, Red was tracking Mr. Noble, the second-grade teacher on lunch duty.

I opened my hand and dropped the spork. "I was fighting this war to protect us," I said, speaking in my warrior voice. "To prevent *her* from coming over here. As soon as *she* sees us, *she's* going to join us. This war would've prevented that. Don't say I didn't warn you."

At that very moment, Tiki bounded out of the lunch line.

"Shields!" I reached for my spork.

Avery smacked my hand again.

Tiki headed our way.

"I warned you," I said.

"I knew you'd be here." She skip-walked up. "You look like booth people."

"All the fifth graders sit in the booths," Avery said.

"Check this out." Tiki slid next to Diego and plopped her tray on the table. "I bet none of you can tell me what this is." She pointed to the top corner of her tray. "Name that food."

Red's hand shot up. "Crunchy baby carrots!" he blurted.

"Ha!" Tiki snort-laughed. "That's exactly what they are!"

Diego thumbed Red. "This one can recite the school menu word for word."

"Cool-a-rino," Tiki said. She picked up her applesauce container, bit the end of the foil tab, and pulled it open. Then she turned to Avery. "Why are you in a wheelchair?"

"Because I can't walk."

"Can any of you do this?" Tiki asked, looking around the table.

She stuck her tongue straight out, bent in the ends, and hooked it back. Then she curled her upper lip so that her tongue touched the tip of her nose.

"What are you doing?" I said.

She tilted her head. "Touching my nose with my tongue."

"Why?"

"Because I can."

I looked at Diego. He was swinging his hat's braided strings, rocking them back and forth. Diego's the only kid at RJE who's allowed to wear a hat. He started wearing hats when he got really sick a couple years ago. He's worn one ever since.

Tiki picked up my spork and pointed to the middle of her tray. "Try naming this food." She wagged the spork at Red. "You can't guess. Not right away."

Red covered his mouth with both hands.

"Something that came out of a dog's butt," Diego said.

Tiki looked at Avery.

"Some type of meat?"

She faced me.

I shrugged.

"Tasty fish taco!" Red burst out.

"Ding, ding, ding!" Tiki said.

"Whatever it is," Diego said, "it's still not as nasty as restaurant mints."

"Dude, you and Danny scarred me for life with your presentation," Avery said.

Last month, the whole class did a project called That's Nasty. Everyone had to work with a partner and do a report on something super gross. Diego and Danny did theirs on restaurant mints, which get touched by so many dirty fingers and have disgusting germs all over them.

"I was named after a whale," Tiki said, dropping my spork back on my lunch tray.

"A whale?" I said.

"Yeppers. Everyone thinks my name is Egyptian, but it's not."

"Dude, how are you named after a whale?" Avery asked.

"My pop is a big animal rights activist. He—"

"Pop?" Avery interrupted.

"That's what she calls her father," I said.

"My pop loves whales. The week I was born, he was reading about this one whale named Takara. *Takara* means 'treasure' in Japanese. That's how I got my name. My parents say I'm a treasure, too." She blew the hair off her forehead and hand-brushed it to the side. "BTW, I always know when we're about to move."

"Move?" I said.

"Yeppers. I always know when we're about to move again."

Avery curled her lip. "Dude, what are you talking about?"

"Pop shaves. Whenever we're about to move again, Pop shaves."

"Why does he shave?" Diego asked.

"It makes things less stressful when we travel. Some people act weird around him when he has his beard. Especially in airports. Shaving days are—"

"You're Muslim?" Avery asked.

"Yeppers," Tiki said. "My mom used to wear a hijab all the time, but not so much anymore."

"What's a hijab?" I asked.

"A head scarf," Diego and Avery said at the same time.

I was surprised they both knew.

"My aunt still wears one," Tiki said. She opened her hands and ran her fingertips over her hair. "She has this one hijab that's navy blue with white circles. That's my favorite. She doesn't shake people's hands, anyone's hands, because—"

"How many schools have you gone to?" I cut her off.

"Eight."

"Eight?" Diego said. "Yo, that's a lot of schools."

Tiki pointed to her lunch. "Why does this school still use foam trays?"

"Because the new food service is the friggin' worst," Avery said.

"Ms. Eunice, Ms. Carmen, Ms. Joan, Ms. Audrey, and Ms. Liz no longer work here," Red said.

"Who are they?"

"The Lunch Bunch," Diego said.

"I miss the Lunch Bunch," Red said. "How are we going to have School Lunch Hero Day without the Lunch Bunch?"

Each spring, RJE celebrates School Lunch Hero Day. The Lunch Bunch come dressed as superheroes, and there's an all-day celebration in the cafeteria. One year, every kid made an apron in art class, and another year, a group of parents formed a band called the Punk Farm Five. The school chorus sang with them.

But now only the little kids get to have art, there's no longer a chorus, and the Lunch Bunch is gone.

"These new lunch ladies are so rude," Avery said.

"I say we blow the lid off this joint!" Tiki smacked the table.

Red flinched.

"The food's unrecognizable," she said, "the trays aren't biodegradable, and the lunch ladies are attitudinal."

"Blow the lid off this joint?" I said. "Who says that?"

"I says that." Tiki looked around the table. "We should do an undercover operation."

"An undercover operation?" Diego scratched his ear under his hat.

"People need to know what's going on," Tiki said. "We need to expose this. We can shoot vids—"

"Dude, no way," Avery said. "Not at RJE."

Red hunched his shoulders and turtled his neck.

"Kids aren't allowed to have cell phones," I said.

"Why not?" Tiki asked.

"It's a long story," I said.

"I like long stories."

I checked Red. By the way his arms were pressing against his sides, I could tell he was tapping his legs—pinky-thumb-pinky-thumb-pinky-thumb—under the table.

"RJE used to be Bring Your Own Device," I said, "but it's not a BYOD school anymore."

"Why not?" Tiki asked.

"Because it's not." I let out a puff. "Can we not talk about this?"

"Zwibble," Tiki said.

"What?" Avery and I said at the same time.

"Out of all my words, that's my fave-a-fave. Zwibble."

"What does it mean?"

"Whatever I want it to." Tiki pumped her eyebrows at me. "I still think we should blow the lid off this joint."

"It's okay," I said to Red, who was swaying. "We're not doing this. No one's getting in trouble."

"We'll do an undercover operation that will bring back the Lunch Bunch," Tiki went on. "Because it stinky-stink-stinks when the people you care about don't stick around. You don't appreciate them until they're gone."

"Who says we didn't appreciate the Lunch Bunch?" I shot her a look and then looked back at Red. "No one's getting in trouble," I said again.

I grabbed the back of my neck and squeezed. I'd known Tiki for less than a day—less than half a day—and I already couldn't stand her.

Just a few hours to go, I told myself. I only had to put up with her a few more hours this afternoon and then it was time for basketball.

I could do this. In a few hours, basketball.

Practice Unexpected

I stepped through the gym doorway with Red and stopped dead in my tracks.

Tiki stood at the foul line directly in front of me.

She was talking with Coach Acevedo, but she wasn't just talking. She was talking *and* dribbling. Coach Acevedo never lets anyone dribble a basketball during a conversation.

Never.

"Takara Eid!" Red pointed. "Takara Eid is here."

Tiki was dribbling with both hands. Not with both hands at the same time, but with her right hand *and* her left hand.

A bunch of kids were shooting around at the hoop in front of the stage, but none were paying attention to the new girl and the coach.

"Rip and Red!" Tiki said, waving with her right hand while still dribbling with her left. She headed our way.

"You didn't say you played basketball," I said.

"You didn't ask."

"What are you doing here, Takara Eid?" Red hopped from foot to foot.

"What does it look like?" She popped a bubble.

Tiki was chewing gum. Coach Acevedo never lets anyone chew gum at basketball practice.

Never.

"I don't think there's room for you on the team this season," I said.

"Of course there is," Coach Acevedo said. He twirled his whistle in one hand and clutched his iPad in the other as he made his way over. "On Clifton United, there's always room for a baller like Tiki."

Baller like Tiki?

"Won't the other teams think you're bending the rules and bringing in a ringer?" I asked.

"Absolutely!" Coach Acevedo bumped Tiki's shoulder. "Do you see the way she handles the rock?" He snatched his whistle. "Let them think what they want."

"On this one team I played for," Tiki said, "I had to bring a copy of my birth certificate to all the games."

She began dribbling behind her back. Left to right, back and forth. Knees bent, shifting her hips, blowing bubbles. Then without stopping, she brought the ball around front and started dribbling between her legs. Left to right, back and forth. Like she was walking in place.

"How'd you learn to dribble like that, Takara Eid?" Red asked.

"Practice, Blake Daniels." She picked up her dribble and smiled. "Practice."

I looked down at her sneakers. She was still wearing the canvas low-tops with the different-colored laces.

"They may not be three-hundred-dollar Air Super Dupers," she said, still smiling, "but they work a-okay-a-roozy for me. They're my good-luck kicks."

"We now have a bunch of ball-handlers on Clifton United," Coach Acevedo said. "Possibilities and opportunities." He nodded to Red. "Go show Tiki what you can do from the foul line."

"I shoot free throws underhanded, Takara Eid," Red said, hopping faster and smiling his super-happy basketball smile.

"Like that old-time basketball player?" she asked.

"Yes!" Red patted the Golden State Warriors logo on the front of his jersey and then spun around and tapped the name across his shoulders. "Rick Barry wore number twenty-four. That's why I wear number twenty-four."

"Red is Clifton United's free-throw-shooting machine," Coach Acevedo said.

"Amaze-balls!" Tiki said. "This I got to see."

Just like that, my best friend and Tiki headed off.

A Whole New Ballgame

Tweet! Tweet!

"Let's circle up!" Coach Acevedo said, waving everyone to center court.

I sprinted over and arrived first. As soon as that whistle blew, my brain shifted into basketball mode. When I'm playing ball, I'm *all* about hoops. That's all my brain focuses on.

Red raced up next to me. We fist-bumped.

"Circle up," Coach Acevedo said. "That's my new phrase for this season. I just finished a book by my favorite coach. It's an expression she used. Circle up."

"Circle up," Red repeated.

"Welcome to Fall Ball Season II," Coach Acevedo said. "We're going to be running things a little bit differently this season. Make that, we're going to be running things a lot bit differently." He twirled his whistle. "For all you new faces here, that won't mean much. But for all you old faces, we don't want anyone getting complacent, and if you don't know what *complacent* means, look it up when you get home."

I was pretty sure I knew what *complacent* meant. It's when you don't practice hard because you think you don't have to.

"This season has a whole new set of rules." Coach Acevedo picked up his iPad and checked the screen. "Once again, for all you newcomers, that won't make a difference. But for my returnees, there are some big changes. For instance, we're no longer playing eight-minute quarters. We're playing twenty-minute halves this season."

I looked around. We were a bigger team than last season. Much bigger. Chris Collins, who attended the tryouts last season but wasn't able to play, was tall and solid. He was definitely going to play down low. So was Dylan Silver. He was even taller than Chris. He reminded me of Shaggy from *Scooby-Doo*.

"Clifton United has four new players," Coach Acevedo said, "but as far as we're concerned, everyone's starting fresh. *Tabula rasa*."

"A Latin phrase meaning 'clean slate,'" Tiki said.

"Exactly," Coach Acevedo said.

Tiki held up her arms and pushed out her hip. "At one of my old schools, we learned a Latin phrase a day. *Carpe diem* means 'seize the day.'"

Coach Acevedo nodded. "It does."

"And the Latin phrase—"

"I'm going to *seize* this moment and keep things moving, Tiki," Coach Acevedo interrupted. "When we played back in September and October, we weren't concerned with wins and losses. Our focus was on growing as a team, which we did. But for this second fall season, we're shifting that focus." He drew a circle in the air with his finger. "Clifton United goes thirteen deep, and we're going to need all thirteen of us in order to win. Yes, *win*. That's how we're shifting our focus. This league is competitive, and we're not just competing. We're winning."

We're winning.

My brain, which was already in basketball mode, shifted into fast-and-furious basketball mode.

When it comes to basketball, I get a little bit competitive. Or to borrow Coach Acevedo's expression, I get a lot bit competitive.

Last season, I was able to keep my crazed competitiveness in check because of Red. It was the first time we'd been able to run ball together, and that was all that really mattered (that and the fact that our team was awful, and we pretty much knew we were going to get our butts kicked every time we took the court).

But last season was the exception.

When I played on select teams in third and fourth grade, I *had* to win every time, and let me tell you, Mom didn't exactly appreciate how seriously I took things. After one game, I had a Fukushima moment, as she called it (I had to look up what that meant). I started crying like a two-year-old, crawled under the bleachers, and refused to move. A parent from the team we'd lost to had to drag me out.

* * *

As soon as drills began, I went into even faster-and-more-furious basketball mode.

Coach Acevedo started us off with a full-court layup drill. Half the team lined up along one baseline, half the team lined up along the other. The first person in each line dribbled the length of the floor full speed and took a layup.

"We're counting on a lot of layup opportunities this season," Coach Acevedo said. "We need to hit those layups every time. Every time starts now."

All thirteen of us had to make our layups. First, we had to make them righty. Then we had to make them lefty. No stopping until we made twenty-six layups in a row.

We were able to make it through the righty layups. But the lefty layups . . .

Tweet! Tweet!

"Looks like we're going to be here awhile," Coach Acevedo said when Wil, the first person to take one, didn't even hit the rim.

Tweet! Tweet!

"Take it from the top," Coach Acevedo said when Mehdi's lefty layup banged off the bottom of the rim and hit him in the forehead.

I can't say Wil and Mehdi were our weak links because everyone was responsible for the restarts.

Well, almost everyone.

I didn't miss a single layup. I was never the reason we had to take it from the top.

Neither was Tiki.

Tiki was a lefty. That was why she could dribble so well with her left and didn't miss a lefty layup. I'd never been on a team with a lefty.

Tweet! Tweet!

"Time to switch things up," Coach Acevedo said, even though we hadn't made the twenty-six straight. "Let's everyone get a partner."

I slid next to Red.

"Since we have an odd number," Coach Acevedo said, "Max, you're with me."

Max was another new player. During lefty layups, he was the one who had missed when we got the closest. When he did, Red was the first to give him a pound. Red was the first to give everyone a pound or high five and say "Good try" or "Shake it off" when they missed their layups.

That's Red.

The next drill was another full-court layup drill, but this drill involved passing. Each pair had to pass the ball back and forth while running down the court. The ball wasn't allowed to hit the floor, and we weren't allowed to travel.

Red and I went first.

"You ready?" I asked.

"Ready as I'll ever be, Mason Irving."

Tweet! Tweet!

"Here come Rip and Red," I play-by-played. "Rip sends it across to Red, Red passes it back. Slide-stepping from the foul line to half-court—that's some good-looking footwork from this duo. Rip passes to Red, Red to Rip. Rip leads Red inside the foul line . . . He shoots . . . It's good!"

"Bam!" Red cheered.

"Boo-yah!" I scooped up the ball. "We need a new handshake."

"Oh, yeah!" Red said. "A new season, a new handshake."

"Let's come up with one this week."

As we waited in line, I studied my teammates. Tiki and Chris fired crisp passes and looked like they'd been playing together for years. Maya and Dylan were in perfect sync, too. Dylan's arms were so long that when he went up for his layup, his fingers brushed the bottom of the backboard. Jason and Wil made it the length of the court with the ball only touching the floor once. Jason sank the layup going up strong.

This Clifton United team had all the pieces: ball-handlers, rebounders, passers, inside scoring threats, shooters. It was just a matter of putting those pieces in place.

"Back come Rip and Red," I announced as we stepped onto the court for our next turn. "These two really look sharp out there. Red across to Rip. Rip back to Red nearing the top of the key. Red to Rip . . . Rip to Red . . . Red back to Rip for the lefty layup . . . bang!"

"Let's circle up," Coach Acevedo said, standing at midcourt after the final drill. "Hustle on over."

No one hustled on over. There was no hustling left to be had. We staggered to midcourt. Max and Maya lay down. Then Jeffrey lay down between them. Then the rest of the team dropped. Except for Red, but only because Red doesn't sit on floors. We'd run more at this practice than we had at all the practices last season combined.

"Wow." Coach Acevedo laughed. "So much for circling

up in a huddle." He clapped and pointed to the stage. "Let's go have a seat up there."

We zombie-walked to the end of the gym, but not everyone made it onto the stage. Max and Jeffrey dropped to the court again. Dylan and Chris sat down beside them.

I sat next to Red, who leaned over the front of the stage. Tiki was on his left.

"Clifton United is going to be in better shape than every other team," Coach Acevedo said. "Conditioning is our key. We're going to run our opponents off the court."

I pounded the stage. "I like the way that sounds!"

"Conditioning takes time," Coach Acevedo said. "Getting in shape is a process. Rome wasn't built in a day."

"Rome wasn't built in a day?" Red made a face. "What does building Rome have to do with conditioning?"

"It's an expression." I nudged his knee. "Things take time."

"Got it."

"On one of my old teams," Tiki said, sliding off the stage, "we pressed the whole game."

My mind flashed back to last season, the first time we played Millwood. They met us on defense in the backcourt and full-court pressed us all game. It was out of control. Their coach was out of control, too. He yelled the whole time; I called him Coach Crazy.

But the second time we played them, we showed them. Red sure did.

"We should have a pressing strategy," Tiki said, still chewing her gum. She stepped next to Coach Acevedo. "Full-court, man-to-man coverage the whole game. We'll be in shape for it."

"It's something to consider," Coach Acevedo said. "Now, when—"

"On my old team," Tiki interrupted, "my coach used this math strategy. That's why we pressed the whole game. You see, there are two time limits in basketball." She crossed her arms and held up her fingers like she was making peace signs. “You have five seconds to get the ball inbounds, and ten seconds to get the ball across midcourt.”

“I learned about that on a sports show!” Red leaped off the stage. “This man had to coach his daughter’s basketball team, but he didn’t know anything about basketball.” He hopped from foot to foot. “So the man used a math strategy and coached the team all the way to the championship!”

“Exacta-rino! That’s where my old coach got the idea.” Tiki pointed her index fingers at Red and moved her arms back and forth like she was dancing. “Forcing turnovers and making layups—that was his strategy. That was our strategy, too.”

“Did you win the championship, Takara Eid?”

“I don’t know.” She shrugged. “We moved before the end of the season.”

I brushed the locks off my forehead and looked away. In a matter of hours, Tiki had taken over my table in class, taken over my booth in the cafeteria, and now she was taking over basketball.

CC and Tiki

"I'm starting Community Circle today with one of *mi abuela*'s sayings," Mr. Acevedo said.

We were all seated in the meeting area. Red and I were on the green polka-dotted beanbag chairs next to the couch. Mr. Acevedo sat cross-legged on the carpet where he always did.

"Before I do," he said, "will someone please bring Tiki up to speed? Explain to her what I'm talking about." He pointed with his chin to Sebi.

"Mr. Acevedo likes to share his grandmother's sayings," Sebi said without looking up from the gargoyle he was doodling on his folder. "They're pieces of advice or words to live by."

"He visits her every summer in the Dominican Republic," Hunter said.

"My family is from the DR," Mr. Acevedo said. "So my grandmother, *mi abuela*, likes to—"

"How many tattoos do you have?" Tiki interrupted.

"Many."

"At one of my old schools," Tiki said, "the teachers weren't allowed to have tattoos. If they did, they had to keep them covered."

Mr. Acevedo nodded. *"En boca cerrada no entran moscas."*

"One of my teachers had to wear gloves," Tiki said, holding out her hands. "She had moons and stars on all her fingers."

Mr. Acevedo nodded again. *"En boca cerrada no entran moscas,"* he repeated.

"A shut mouth doesn't catch flies," Diego said, swinging his hat strings.

"Pretty close," Mr. Acevedo said.

"Flies don't enter a shut mouth," Christine said.

"Excellent." Mr. Acevedo recrossed his legs and grabbed his ankles. "So what do you think that means?" He chin-pointed to Xander.

"If you don't speak, you can't say anything bad," he said.

"That's pretty close, too, X," Mr. Acevedo said.

Tiki's hand shot up. She waved it like a kindergartner.

Mr. Acevedo called on her.

"The school where my teacher had the moons and stars tattooed on her fingers also had a dress code," she said.

"I'd be in trouble if RJE enforced the teacher dress code." Mr. Acevedo chuckled.

Mr. Acevedo always wore the same pair of jeans. He told us that the first day. But he always changed his shirt, socks, and underwear. He told us that, too.

"You weren't allowed to wear jackets, hats, or gloves during the school day." Tiki snort-laughed. "So one rule said my teacher had to keep her tattoos covered, and another rule said she couldn't wear gloves!"

"Thanks, Tiki." Mr. Acevedo brushed the hair off his face. "My grandmother's expression makes me think of the word *discretion*. If you don't know what *discretion* means, look it up."

I definitely knew what *discretion* meant. Mom used the word all the time. It means think before you do or say something.

"I have an aunt," Mr. Acevedo said, "who has a habit of sticking her foot in her mouth."

Red grabbed his ankle, lifted his leg, and smiled.

"She says the most inappropriate things," Mr. Acevedo said. "It always makes everyone around her incredibly uncomfortable. Good judgment—discretion—is an important character trait. It's one of—"

"So do you know what my teacher did?" Tiki interrupted again. "She—"

"One mic, Tiki," Mr. Acevedo said, cutting her off. He spoke firmly. "We speak with one mic in Room 208." He held up a finger. "We don't interrupt others when they're speaking."

I covered my smirk. Tiki wasn't taking over CC.

Operation Food Fight

"She's lying," I said, picking the cheese off my pizza. "I don't believe a word she says."

"Why would she make things up?" Diego asked.

"Who cares?"

"She's been to eight schools, Mason Irving," Red said.

"No way."

Diego, Red, and I were at lunch, sitting at the same booth as yesterday. Diego was across from me. Red was on my left.

"She always has a story," I said. "About one of her old teachers, about one of her old schools, about one of her old teams." I tilted back my head and dropped the cheese into my mouth. "Everything."

"She cracks me up," Diego said. "I like that she says whatever's on her mind."

I checked the kitchen area. In a matter of seconds, Tiki would be heading our way. At least today, she couldn't . . .

Tiki burst off the lunch line.

"Here she comes," I muttered.

"We're becoming a thing," she said, walking up. She slid next to me and tapped the fruit dish in the corner of her tray. "Name that food."

"We're not playing that today," I said.

"Oh, okay." She shrugged. "Not to be gross-hoppers, but check this out."

She held up her thumb. She'd bitten off most of the nail and had chewed the cuticle until it was red and scabby.

"Sweet!" Diego said.

"Sweet!" Red repeated.

I looked over at the first and second graders seated at the long tables. The girl at the end of one table was so small her light-up sneakers didn't reach the floor. The boy across from her wearing the Perry the Platypus shirt was even tinier.

I didn't think I was ever going to get used to eating with the little kids.

"So I started planning our operation," Tiki said.

"What operation?" I said.

"Rip," she whined. "The operation from yesterday, remember?" She swatted my arm. "We're blowing the lid off this joint."

"There is no operation."

"It's a mission, not an operation," Diego said while chewing. "When I think of operations, I think of doctors cutting me open." He spit the food back onto his tray.

"That was pretty," I said.

"I can't eat that." He wiped his tongue with his fingers. "That's supposed to be pizza, but that's not pizza. That's even worse than hospital pizza."

"A mission it is," Tiki said. "Now we need a name for our mission." She took a bite of her slice.

Diego raised his spork. "The Undercover Lunch Ninjas."

"Oh, yeah, Diego Vasquez!" Red said, his knees bouncing. "The Undercover Lunch Ninjas. I like that. I like that a lot."

"The Undercover Lunch Ninjas are here to save RJE." Diego jabbed his spork into the table. "Better food, better service, better days."

"Ew," Tiki said, spitting out her pizza and patting her tongue with a napkin. "That's definitely not pizza."

"I told you," Diego said.

"It's not that bad," I said, even though all I was able to eat was the cheese.

"It's not that bad," Red said.

He was eating his pizza like he always ate pizza. First, he peeled off the crust. Then he ate the toppings, cheese, and sauce. In that order. Then he ate the bread. Except for the crust. Red never ate the crust.

"Here's what I'm thinking for the mission," Tiki said. She put her tray on the floor and clasped her hands on the table. "We'll run it a few times. On different days, when they're serving different foods."

"Definitely on a pizza day," Diego said.

"Yeppers, yeppers. We need at least four or five of us. We'll each have a different role."

"We'll need lookouts," Diego said.

"Ooh, I love it when a plan comes together." Tiki unclasped her hands and rubbed them. "That's what this guy always says on this old TV show my pop loves." She pointed across the cafeteria. "Hey, there's the girl in the wheelchair. What's her name again?"

"Avery Goodman," Red said.

"Avery!" Tiki shouted. She stood and waved her arms wildly, and for a second, she looked like one of those inflatable air dancers you see in front of a car dealership. "Avery!"

Avery wheeled over and hockey-stopped at our booth.

"I totally forgot your name," Tiki said, smacking her cheeks. "Red had to tell me. I'm really, really sorry, but you know how it is. I meet so many kids and . . . Please don't be mad." She touched Avery's armrest. "It's the worst-o-worst when I can't remember the names of the kids I'm friends with."

Friends?

"Whatever, dude," Avery said. She dropped her lunch bag onto the table. "It's fine."

"Groovalicious," Tiki said.

I rolled my eyes.

I didn't use to roll my eyes. I picked that up from Avery.

It's so weird that we're friends now. If you'd told me at the beginning of school that Avery and I would be friends, I would've said not in a gazillion years. No friggin' way.

Friggin'. That's Avery's word.

"BTW, I was in a wheelchair once," Tiki said.

We all looked at her.

"One time, we were at the airport, and there was a volleyball team waiting at our gate. They all found wheelchairs and started playing right there. Bumping and setting and spiking. So I played, too."

"They let you?" Avery took out her lunch.

"Yeppers. But I knocked into this guy wearing a suit and he spilled coffee all over himself." She smacked her palm against her forehead. "Embarrassment city! My pop was not happy. No siree bob."

"Since when did you start bringing lunch?" Diego asked Avery.

"Since they stopped serving pizza on pizza days." She motioned to the trays. "That is not pizza."

"Hot-to-trot!" Tiki touched Avery's armrest again and then reached across the table and tapped Diego's elbow. "That's exactly what we said."

I looked at Diego. He was wearing his black-and-white knit hat with the dog's face on top. Whenever he tilted his head, it looked like the huge brown eyes were staring into your soul.

"This is my protest." Avery held up her chicken salad sandwich. "I'm boycotting pizza days until they start serving pizza again. I want last year's pizza again."

"That was good pizza, Avery Goodman," Red said.

"Operation Food Fight!" Tiki blurted. "That's what we should call our mission."

"Sweet!" Diego said. "I like that."

"Wait a sec," I said to Diego. "A minute ago you said operations made you think about doctors cutting you open."

"They do," Diego said. "But I like that name a lot. Operation Food Fight."

"Operation Food Fight," Red repeated. "I like that name a lot, too, Diego Vasquez."

"What are you four talking about?" Avery peeled the crust off her sandwich.

"The operation we're planning," Tiki answered.

"What operation?"

"Our undercover operation," Tiki said. "We're going to run it on different days when they're serving different foods. One of the days will be a pizza day. Some of us will be—"

"What's the operation?" Avery said, cutting her off. "Just say it."

"We're going to blow the lid off this joint, remember? We're going to show everyone what's really happening in the cafeteria. We're going to take vids of what's—"

"Stop, Tiki!" I interrupted. "How many times do we have to say it to you? We're not allowed to have cell phones. Don't you listen?"

"I listen." She snort-laughed. "If we get caught with a cell phone or shooting cell-phone vids, we get sent to the electric chair and the guillotine."

"Not funny."

I checked Red. His shoulders were hunched, and he was pinky-thumb-tapping his leg. I placed my hand on top of his.

"Anyway," Tiki said, flexing her eyebrows, "who said anything about a cell phone?"

"I still don't get it," Avery said.

"What don't you get?" Tiki asked.

"What do you hope to accomplish?"

"Rip?" Tiki pointed her index finger at me like she was aiming a gun. Then she lowered her thumb like she was pulling the trigger. "Tell her, Rip."

"Don't look at me," I said.

"I'm looking at you." She flexed her eyebrows again. "I can see that mind of yours working."

I lifted my hand from Red's, which was no longer tapping his leg. "No, you can't," I said.

"You're the brains behind the mission."

"No, I'm not."

"Let's pretend that you are."

"Let's not."

"Let's pretend that you are." Tiki placed her elbows on the table and rested her cheeks in her hands. "What should be our goal?"

"We want the Lunch Bunch back," Diego said.

"Excellent-a-mundo." Tiki still looked at me. "Instead of a cell phone, we'll use an action camera to shoot the vids. Like a GoPro."

"Dude, where are we going to get one of those?" Avery asked.

"X's brother," Diego said. "He has, like, ten."

"Seven," Red said, relaxing his shoulders. "Xander McDonald's older brother has seven action cameras. Last month, Xander McDonald's older brother helped us with the video for our project."

"I just love it when a plan comes together," Tiki said.

"That's what some guy says on some old TV show your pop loves." I rolled my eyes. "Anyway, X's brother isn't going to just let us use one of his cameras."

"Sure he will." Diego patted his chest. "If I ask him."

Diego's family and Xander's family were best friends.

"Fantabulous!" Tiki said. She turned to Avery. "You're our secret weapon. Every mission needs a secret weapon."

"Whatever, dude."

"We'll attach the camera to the back of your chair," Tiki said. "No one will notice it."

Diego nodded along. "That's tight."

"This is such a bad idea," I said. "We're going to get in so much trouble for this."

"No, we're not," Tiki said.

"You don't know what you're talking about," I snapped. "We're not allowed to have cell phones, and before you say the camera isn't a cell phone, we're using it like a cell-phone camera, and that's exactly how the kids last year got . . ."

I didn't finish. Red's fists were tapping his cheeks, and his knees were bouncing against the table.

I let out a puff and looked from Avery to Diego. "I can't believe you're going along with this."

"Listen, Rip." Tiki held out her hands. "I'm the new girl, she's in a wheelchair, you're the teacher's pet, he's—"

"I'm not the teacher's pet," I said, cutting her off.

"Okay." Tiki snort-laughed. "You're not the teacher's pet. You're Mr. Perfect." She winked at Diego. "He's the cutie pie with the doggy hat. Red's Red. We're the good kids. I've been to so many schools. I know how this works. We're not getting in trouble. Now, who's down with Operation Food Fight?"

Clean or Dirty?

"Which is it?" Mom asked, holding up my red basketball shorts. "Clean or dirty?"

"Dirty," I said.

She dropped them onto the pile of clothes by my door. "What about these?" She held up my blue-and-white-striped boxers.

"Dirty."

I was sitting on my bed with my back against the wall, shooting my Nerf into the air. I was practicing my form—spreading my fingers, relaxing my wrist, holding my follow-through, watching the rotation—as we sorted the clothes that had taken over my room.

Or should I say, as Mom sorted the clothes.

"What about this shirt?" She sniffed my ThunderCats tee and tossed it onto the pile before I could answer. Then she grabbed the folded sheets off the floor. "Rip, is this the clean bedding I gave you on Sunday?"

"Yeah."

"Yes?"

I smiled. "Uh-huh."

Mom doesn't like it when I say "yeah" or "uh-huh." She doesn't like it when I nod instead of speaking either.

She put the sheets on my worktable and plucked the Nerf out of the air. "Until all this is sorted," she said, pointing the ball at the clothes by my closet and then at the heap on the chair beside my bed, "and at least three loads are washed, dried, folded, and put away, there's no password."

"That's so not fair," I half whined.

"No, *this* isn't fair." She pointed again. "No password."

That's Mom's new thing. She changes the Wi-Fi password and holds it hostage. She learned this *strategy* from one of the teachers at her school. Mom's the principal at River West, a public middle school in a district a few towns over.

"We can put the first load in together," she said.

"C'mon, Mom."

"We can do it tomorrow instead of going to basketball, if you like." She flipped the ball onto my bed. "Rip, this shows no responsibility whatsoever."

"Is this where you say I'm not ready for a dog?"

"Looks like I don't have to."

I reached for the Nerf. "Irving for three," I announced as I shot the ball at the hoop above my closet. "Splash! Nothing but net."

"So tell me more about the new girl," Mom said. "What's her name?"

"Tiki."

When I'd gotten home from school yesterday, I told Mom we had a new girl in class, but of course, she already knew. Lesley Irving knows about everything at RJE. All the parents know she's a principal, so they're always emailing and texting her questions or asking her for school advice. Mom doesn't mind because it keeps her in the loop.

Sometimes a little too much in the loop, if you ask me.

"She says the weirdest things," I said.

"How so?"

"She just does."

"Honey, you're going to have to explain yourself a little better than that." Mom picked up the laundry basket from the floor.

"She likes to make up her own words. She has her own vocabulary."

Mom held out the basket and nodded to the compression socks and T-shirts on my pillow. "She's just trying to fit in."

"By making up her own language?" I scooped up the clothes and dropped them in. "She said she's been to eight schools, but I don't believe her. No one moves around that much."

"Honey, the population around here is much more transient than it used to be. Kids are coming and going all the time. You see that."

"I know." I grabbed my purple teddy bear by the arm and pulled him onto my knee.

"I can't imagine how difficult it must be for her." She placed the basket on my worktable and sat down on the bed. "That poor girl."

"She's from Egypt."

Mom flicked a piece of lint out of my hair.

I ducked away. "She said that whenever her family moves, her dad shaves his beard so people won't act weird around him in airports."

"Such a shame." She reached behind her and pulled a book out from between the mattress and the wall. "You looking for this?"

"There it is."

A Wrinkle in Time.

I had started reading it for Choice, but I stopped after a few chapters. *A Wrinkle in Time* is one of those books we're supposed to like, but I didn't. I couldn't get into it. But then Mr. Acevedo gave me the graphic novel version, and let me tell you, even though I'm a slo-mo reader, I was blowing through it. I was already up to the part where they go into the central intelligence building.

"This book is always getting banned," Mom said, fanning the pages. "Someone somewhere is always trying to keep it out of the hands of kids."

"That's why I wanted to read it."

I love reading books that grown-ups don't want kids to read. But the thing is, after I read them, I never really understand why they don't want us to read them.

"Let's get started on this laundry." Mom swatted my leg with the book. "So you can go to basketball tomorrow."

The Strategy

Tweet! Tweet!

"Let's circle up, Clifton United," Coach Acevedo said at the beginning of practice the next day. "Time for a little speech."

Tweet! Tweet!

"I'm usually not a big fan of talking at practices," he said, once everyone had gathered under the hoop by the stage. "I much prefer practicing at practice. But before we get started today, I need about three minutes." He waved the magazine he was holding. "Thanks to Tiki over here, I did some homework."

Red's hand shot up. "You're not a big fan of homework, Coach Acevedo," he said.

"No, I'm not, Red. But I am a big fan of learning on our own. We always need to be curious."

"Be curious," Red whispered.

"I read about that math strategy Tiki mentioned."

"My old team's strategy!" She held up her hands and pushed her hip out to the side. "Thank you. Thank you very much." She bowed several times.

"I also watched that sports show Red mentioned."

"Oh, yeah!" Red hopped.

"We've got some serious talent on this squad," Coach Acevedo said, "but so do the teams we'll be facing. In fact, some of our opponents are loaded. So after crunching some numbers, I've decided this unorthodox strategy just may give Clifton United our best shot at winning, and if you don't know what *unorthodox* means, look it up when you get home."

I was pretty sure I knew what *unorthodox* meant: unusual.

Coach Acevedo opened to the article. "This gentleman right here knew next to nothing about basketball." He pointed to a photograph of a man wearing a suit. "But he understood mathematics. So he came up with a strategy based on the mathematics of basketball. And it worked."

"It worked for my team, too," Tiki said.

"You told us," I muttered.

"Now, we're not following his strategy step by step," Coach Acevedo continued, "but we are going to use his approach as our model. We're going to force turnovers, make layups, and run our opponents out of the gym. Like I said Monday, everyone on Clifton United will need to contribute this season."

"I like the way that sounds!" Tiki shouted.

I like the way that sounds.

I grabbed the locks above my neck. That's what I'd said on Monday. Exactly what I'd said.

Tweet! Tweet!

"Let's get running."

Sprinting

Clifton United stood on the baseline and waited for the next whistle. We were running up-and-backs. That's what the drill was called. On my select team, we called it by a different name, but Coach Acevedo didn't like that name.

"I want to see everyone running like Rip this time," he said.

Running like Rip.

I liked the way that sounded. Make that, I loved the way that sounded.

As soon as Coach had finished his talk, I shifted right into firing-on-all-cylinders-revved-up basketball mode. No way was anyone beating me today. No way.

Tweet! Tweet!

We burst from the baseline.

Sprint to the foul line. Sprint back.

Sprint to half-court. Sprint back.

Sprint to the far foul line. Sprint back.

Sprint to the other baseline. Sprint back.

I finished first.

Again.

"One more time!" Coach Acevedo shouted. "Run like Rip."

Tweet! Tweet!

I was running like Rip, too. Like Rip Hamilton. He played for the Detroit Pistons back in the day. He was known as the Running Man. That's how I got my nickname. Mom says I run around like the Energizer Bunny. I had to YouTube the Energizer Bunny to know what she was talking about.

I finished first.

Again.

"Last set!" Coach Acevedo called. "We go hard!"

Tweet! Tweet!

I won again. Undefeated.

"You can't lose, Mason Irving!" Red panted. "You're Clifton United's up-and-back running machine!" He held out his fist.

I swatted it with my fingers and then clasped my hands behind my head and took long breaths. "We definitely need a new handshake."

"Keep pushing your teammates, Rip," Coach Acevedo said as we lined up for the next drill. "Keep setting the tone. Lead the way."

Fine by me.

The next conditioning drill was the zigzag drill. Last season when we tried running this, instead of pivoting and sliding the length of the court, Clifton United stumbled over the mini-cones, knocked one another down, and ran in every direction but the correct one. Before we started today, Coach Acevedo showed us what the drill looked like on his iPad.

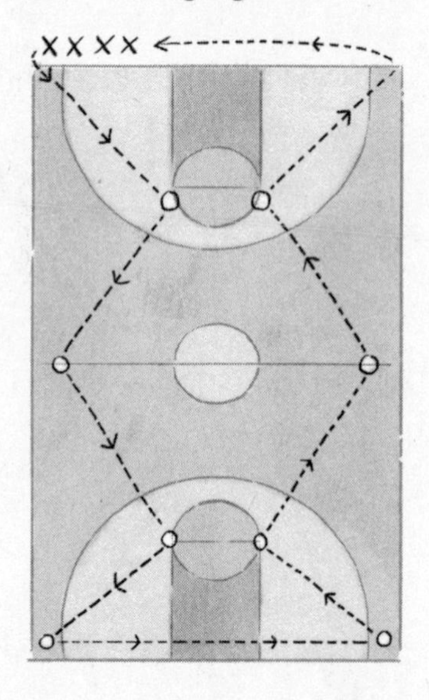

"We run this drill in defensive stances, pivoting and sliding," he explained.

Everyone said they knew what to do, but I could tell everyone didn't. So it was time to lead the way. Just like Coach Acevedo wanted. It was . . .

"I see you, Rip," Tiki said, lining up behind me. She blew a bubble and popped it. "I'm coming for you."

"What?" I made a face. I still couldn't believe Coach Acevedo was letting her chew gum during practice.

"I'm coming for you." She pointed two fingers at her eyes and then pointed them at me. "I'm passing you."

I looked around. She had me on blast. Everyone heard.

"That's not what this drill is about," I said. "You're not supposed to pass me."

"Then don't let me." She snort-laughed again.

No way was she passing me. No way.

Tweet! Tweet!

She didn't pass me. Just like I said she wouldn't.

"Way to set the tone out there, Rip," Coach Acevedo said. "Way to lead the way."

Short and Sweet

During outdoor recess the next day, Red and I came up with our handshake.

"You ready?" I asked, taking off my hoodie.

Red took off his. "Ready as I'll ever be, Mason Irving," he said.

Roll the arms and dance to the left.
Roll the arms and dance to the right.
Slap hands with the right.
Slap hands with the left.
Jumping hip bump.
Then on the landing . . .
"Boo-yah!"

"Short and sweet," I said.

"Short and sweet, Mason Irving!"

Last season, our handshake had fourteen steps. This season, we were going with short and sweet.

“One more time?” I said.

“Oh, yeah!”

Pizza and Pushing the Envelope

I placed *A Wrinkle in Time* on my chest, leaned back in the bathtub, and looked around the classroom.

Like always during Choice, everyone was reading.

The OMG girls sat on the couch, their legs woven together like they were playing Twister.

Avery was parked underneath the writing-binders shelf by the door.

Red, Xander, Hunter, Declan, Danny, and Zachary had the beanbag chairs. They sat in the corner by the Yo! Read This! board, next to where Mr. Acevedo had posted the QR codes for the classroom iPads that linked to the author websites and book trailers for the recommended titles.

Mr. Acevedo was reading, too. He sat on the windowsill behind his desk, wearing his Do Not Disturb sign.

I checked the board and reread the message that had been waiting for us when we walked in:

TODAY'S MENU

1st Course: Choice

2nd Course: Community Circle

3rd Course: T3 in the Amp

I hoped the first course on the menu would be the longest. I lifted the book off my chest and went back to Meg, Charles Wallace, and Calvin.

"Let's put away our reading and head to the meeting area," Mr. Acevedo said about twenty minutes later.

I popped out of the tub like a jack-in-the-box, flung my book in the direction of my desk (it slid off and landed on the floor), and dashed for the couch. I snagged the middle seat between Red and Attie.

"Let's talk about lunch," Mr. Acevedo said after everyone had settled in. He sat cross-legged in his spot on the carpet. "Today's pizza day."

"Tuesday's pizza day," I said, correcting him.

"So is today," Olivia said. "Weren't you listening during announcements?"

No, I wasn't. I never listen to the announcements, and the only time I check the announcement monitor in the main hall is when one of my friends is on it or it's showing a sports clip.

"Pizza with grilled chicken topping, mixed vegetable medley, chilled tropical fruit, and salad," Red said, reciting the menu.

"Pizza Darling!" I said, suddenly remembering that Tuesday's lunch had been named after the principal.

"More like Pizza Disgusting," Avery said. "That pizza is friggin' foul."

"You're telling me," Noah said, wiping the side of his mouth with his palm.

"So we're really having leftovers for lunch today," Hunter said.

"I didn't bring my lunch." Avery squeezed her brakes. "What am I going to eat?"

"You have to do something about this, Mr. A.," Danny said.

Mr. Acevedo grabbed his ankles. "What do you want me to do?"

"Get them to serve us real pizza," Declan said. "Use some magic food powers, Teach."

"I'm with Avery," Olivia said. "If I'd known about the menu change, I would've brought my lunch."

"Same," Miles said.

"Me, too." Piper nodded.

"You know things are bad when kids won't eat the pizza on pizza days." Mr. Acevedo chuckled. He tucked his hair behind his ears. "But if you don't like the way things are—"

"Why is pizza day on Tuesday?" Tiki interrupted.

"Not sure." Mr. Acevedo regrabbed his ankles and looked back at Miles and Piper. "If you don't like the way things are, do something about it. Figure out a way to express your dissatisfaction constructively."

"How?" Piper asked.

"I'm not the one who's dissatisfied."

"At all my old schools," Tiki said, "pizza days were always on Friday."

"One thing you can do is gather some evidence," Mr. Acevedo said. "Get some proof. Maybe keep a count of how many kids are bringing lunch on pizza days. Or track the amount of pizza being thrown away. Come up with numbers. Share it."

Gather some evidence. Get some proof. Share it.

I checked Avery and Diego, seated beside the bathtub. I could tell they were thinking the same thing. It was almost as if Mr. Acevedo was giving us *permission* to do Operation Food Fight. Almost.

"The new food service got rid of the composting bins," Olivia said. "They need to bring them back."

"Especially on pizza days," Avery added.

Last year, the Lunch Bunch had us sort our trash. There were three huge bins in the cafeteria—one for landfill garbage like plastic bags, foam cups, and wrappers; one for recyclables like metal, glass, plastic, and milk cartons; and one for food scraps. There was also a red bucket where we had to pour out milk. At first, it was a pain, but after a few days, it wasn't at all.

This year, garbage, recyclables, and food scraps all went into the same can.

"I'm serious about this," Mr. Acevedo said. "Figure out ways to express your dissatisfaction. Sometimes we need to push the—"

"We should get them to move pizza day," Tiki interrupted again.

"One mic, Tiki," Mr. Acevedo said with an edge. He held up a finger. "Remember what I told you the other day. We speak with one mic in Room 208. We don't cut people off."

Tiki covered her mouth with both hands. "Sorry," she said through her fingers.

"It's okay." Mr. Acevedo nodded once. "As I was saying, sometimes in order to effect change, you have to push the envelope."

"The envelope?" Red said. "What envelope?"

"It's an expression, Red," Mr. Acevedo answered before I did. "An idiom. If you don't know what an *idiom* is, look it up. And if you don't know what *pushing the envelope* means, look that up, too."

I knew what *pushing the envelope* meant. It's when you keep putting more and more dirty clothes on your bedroom floor because your mom hasn't threatened to take away your Wi-Fi password.

I wasn't sure about an *idiom*. A type of expression?

"We're going to head outside to the amphitheater in a few for T3," Mr. Acevedo said, hopping to his feet. "But before we do, we need to take a break. We've been sitting for way too long. Let's take ten. Stretch your legs, jump around, dance with someone, do whatever. Then we'll go out."

Read Aloud

The class sat huddled close together on the top two benches of the Amp. It was definitely the coldest day of the fall so far, and everyone either had their hoodies up, their hands dug deeply into their pockets, or both. I sat next to Red. Diego was on the other side of him.

Mr. Acevedo was the only one not sitting. He walked back and forth along a middle bench as he read from the picture book.

"November is picture-book month in Room 208," Mr. Acevedo had announced last Friday at CC. "From now until Thanksgiving, I'll be reading you at least a picture book a day."

Each day before T3, he wrote the same sentence on the board:

That's the banner that's been scrolling across the top of the class webpage all month.

Mr. Acevedo read all different kinds of picture books—funny ones, biographies, historical fiction, even wordless picture books. Yeah, you can read a wordless picture book out loud. At least Mr. Acevedo can. So far, the one with the boy drawing pictures of animals on his sketchpad was my fave.

Mr. Acevedo started T3 today by reading a nonfiction book about this famous mathematician who never really fit in and ended up traveling all over the world. It reminded me of the Albert Einstein book he read to us last week.

Right now, Mr. Acevedo was reading *Rooting for You* by Susan Hood. He said it was one of his favorite picture books, but Mr. Acevedo says that about a lot of picture books. It's about this little seed that's scared to grow from the ground and deal with the world, but I'm pretty certain it's not just about a seed.

I don't think little kids get all the things in picture books, and I'm beginning to think that's how it's supposed to be. Like Mr. Acevedo says . . .

U r never 2 old 4 picture books.

Rookie of the Year

At Saturday morning practice, Coach Acevedo had us running from the first whistle.

Tweet! Tweet!

"Everyone on the baseline! Let's go! Up-and-backs!"

But this time, we dribbled as we ran. Going hard up with the right hand. Going hard back with the left.

Of course, I was in total basketball mode, but I was also in friendly trash-talking mode, and since I was running next to Red, he was on the receiving end.

"You can't keep up with me, Daniels," I said as we waited for the next whistle. "Why do you even bother to run?"

"We'll see," Red said, smiling.

"We'll see?" I laughed mockingly. "That's all you got for me? I'm going to lap you this time, Daniels."

Red shook his fists by his cheeks. "One time . . . one time, Mason Irving, you're going to trip and fall, and when you do . . . when you do, I'm going to step on you. Crush you like a cockroach!"

Tweet! Tweet!

I charged out to a lead. "You're too slow!" I said.

"Keep talking," Red said.

I raced around the first cone and passed Red going in the opposite direction. "You're never going to catch me!" I said. "I may lap you, Daniels!"

But Red was keeping things a lot closer than I thought he would. He knew it, too, which explained his basketball smile. I loved seeing Red having this much fun, having this much fun *with me* on a basketball court.

"Wait until we play Xbox later," Red said after the set.

"I'm going to beat you in Horse. Like I always do, Mason Irving!"

"Video games?" I laughed and swatted the air. "That's the best you got, Daniels?"

Red hopped from foot to foot. "I always beat you in Horse."

"You're comparing this to video games? You're seriously buggin' if—"

Tweet! Tweet!

"And they're off!" I play-by-played the next set. "Red dribbles out to a surprising early lead, but will he be able to hold off Irving once he starts dribbling with his left?"

I sped up, executed a Rip Hamilton–like change of direction at midcourt, and blew by him.

"Irving takes the lead!" I announced. "Oh, Red's in trouble now! Irving is toying with him. A man competing against a boy, a wizard against a muggle. What a dominant performance by Clifton United's all-world, starting point guard."

When Red reached the baseline, I was waiting with my hand on a hip, tapping my foot. "Who's your daddy?" I said.

Red laughed. "You're Clifton United's up-and-back running machine!"

"Handshake?"

"Oh, yeah, Mason Irving!"

For the first time, we busted out our new handshake at basketball.

"Roll left," we chanted. "Roll right. Slap right, slap left." We jumped, bumped hips, and on the landing shouted, "Boo-yah!"

* * *

"Let's circle up, Clifton United," Coach Acevedo said.

We huddled near midcourt.

"Time to shift gears. Time for a contact drill." He pointed his whistle at Red. "You're with me."

Red hustled over next to him.

"For those of you new to Clifton United," Coach Acevedo said, "this is the only time I'm going to address this. Red over here doesn't like physical contact." He placed his arm around Red's shoulder.

Red tensed but didn't squirm away. A few weeks ago, he would have. A few months ago, he would have bugged.

"So Red doesn't participate in contact drills," Coach Acevedo said. "Or, I should say, Red participates *differently* because he will participate in this next drill." He drew a circle in the air with his finger. "Everyone contributes."

"Red is Clifton United's free-throw-shooting machine!" Tiki blurted. She hopped from foot to foot like Red.

I rolled my eyes.

"Thanks, Tiki," Coach Acevedo said. "Now, enough with all this talking. Let's get poppin'. Two lines underneath the basket."

We raced over. I was first in one line. Tiki was first in the other.

"This is an excellent drill for finishing strong around the basket and playing through contact," Coach Acevedo said. "Here's how it works: Two people lie down on their stomachs under the baskets. Red over here is my shooter."

"I'm the shooter." Red patted his chest. "Thanks, Coach Acevedo."

"Red, you start out on the wing by the three-point line and dribble around. After a few seconds, take a shot." He pointed his whistle at the rest of us. "As soon as that ball leaves his hand, everyone yells, 'Shot!' On three, let's give it a whirl. One, two, three . . ."

"Shot!"

"That's what we want to hear all season. Every time an opposing player takes a shot, we're yelling 'shot.' It helps keep everyone involved and focused."

"That's what you wrote on the website," Tiki said. She held up her arms and pushed out her hip.

"That's exactly what I wrote, Tiki. I'm glad you took the time to read my post." Coach Acevedo pointed his index fingers at Tiki and me. "My two point guards, you're my first victims. On the floor. When your teammates say 'shot,' that's your cue. You're on your feet. Battle for the board, battle for the basket. You go until one of you makes a layup. Whatever it takes."

"Whatever it takes?" I shook out my hair.

"I'm not calling fouls." Coach Acevedo twirled his whistle. "But let's not get too crazy. No tripping, elbowing, drop-kicking, or undercutting."

I shook my tingling hands and feet, took a few quick breaths, and dropped to the floor. Then I looked at Tiki. I half expected her to be flailing around like a goldfish out of its bowl or lying on her back instead of her stomach, pretending to make snow angels. But she wasn't. She was on the ground in ready position.

Tweet! Tweet!

Red began to dribble. His smile grew as he swung around the top of the key to the far side of the court.

"Any day now, Red," Coach Acevedo said. "Take that shot."

He took the three-pointer.

"Shot!"

I sprang to my feet and tracked the ball. Red's shot was only going to graze the front rim. I shoulder-bumped Tiki toward the baseline and widened my stance. But instead of jumping for the ball, I turned my hip so that Tiki couldn't get around me. I caught the rock, dribbled once to my right, and shot the off-balance baby jumper.

"Boo-yah!" I hammer-fisted the air as the ball dropped through the hoop.

"Well done, Rip." Coach Acevedo slide-stepped over and gave me a pound. "Love the energy, love the intensity."

I couldn't have hidden my smile if I tried.

"Same two," Coach Acevedo said. He pointed Tiki and me back to the floor. "Run it again."

We dropped to our stomachs.

"I'm Rookie of the Year," Tiki said.

"What?"

"Rookie of the Year. I'm Clifton United's Rookie of the Year." She winked and cracked her gum. "Neat-o, right?"

Tweet! Tweet!

This time, Red shot the ball as soon as Coach Acevedo blew the whistle.

"Shot!"

"Irving leaps to his feet," I play-by-played in my head. "The shot clips the bottom of the backboard, and Tiki reaches the ball first. Oh! Irving chops it out of her hands . . . The ball's loose. Irving's got it. He lowers his shoulder and checks Tiki to the side. Coach Acevedo's really letting these two play. Irving dribbles toward the hoop and goes up for the layup. Oh! Tiki ties him up. Irving muscles up another shot . . ."

Swish!

"Boss!" I grunt-shouted. I pounded my chest and flexed like a defensive back after a sack, not that I looked anything like a defensive back. "I'm a basketball boss!"

"Great work, Rip," Coach Acevedo said. "The Gnat is back!"

Gnat.

Coach Acevedo called me Gnat. That's what the other teams called me when I played third-grade select because when I played defense, I was annoying. Like a gnat.

"One more time, you two." Coach Acevedo pointed to the court again. "Go hard."

A second later, I was back on the floor next to Tiki.

"This is superific fun," she said, touching my wrist.

I pulled it away.

"I just love how hard you're trying." She cracked her gum again. "If I didn't know any better, I would think you were trying to start a fight."

I glared.

"I really am going to win Rookie of the Year," she said, "don't you think?"

Was she trying to get inside my head? Was this her weird way of trash-talking? If it was, it wasn't working. It was just weird.

"Okay, Tiki," I mumbled.

"Okay, what?" She snort-laughed. "Zwibble."

"What?"

She flexed her eyebrows. "That's my fave-a-fave word, remember?"

I let out a puff. It was time to teach the Rookie of the Year she wasn't the Most Valuable Player.

Tweet! Tweet!

Once again, Red put up his shot right away.

"Shot!"

We both jumped up. This time, Tiki went right at me and boxed me out as the ball hit the back iron and popped straight into the air. She was in perfect position for the rebound, but as soon as she leaped for it, I shoved her in the back. She still caught the ball, but not in position for a layup.

"Now what?" I said, shoving her again.

She dribbled right but then spun left and blew past me.

"Ooh!" a few kids shouted.

She had an open look. She was going to score. She flipped up the shot. The ball danced along the lip of the rim . . .

Somehow, it didn't go in.

"Oh!" kids shouted.

We both leaped for the rebound. This time, I grabbed it. I put the ball on the floor, went left, and then Rip

Hamilton–like changed direction. But Tiki stayed with me. Using my shoulder and elbow, I bodied her away so I could put up a layup.

It went in.

"Boo-yah!" I hammer-fisted the air. "Mason Irving, MVP!"

Working Me

"Honey, I really need you to sit still," Mom said.

I was trying to, but I was only wearing thin shorts, and the MacBook on my lap had gone from warm to dag-this-is-getting-really-hot.

We were in the basement watching the Chargers and the Broncos. I was on the floor, Mom was on the couch behind me. She was relocking my hair. She hadn't in several weeks, and she was tired of picking out the lint and telling me it looked ratty.

I was tired of it, too.

I reached for her phone on the sofa cushion.

"How many screens do you need?" she said.

"You're the one who asked me about the Eagles game."

"There's a computer in your lap."

"I'm looking at something."

"Honey, all you're doing is refreshing the same page."

I was on the Clifton United webpage. Coach Acevedo was posting the schedule this evening, and I couldn't wait to see who we were playing.

I checked the phone. "Thirty-four carries, a hundred seventy-two yards, and two touchdowns," I said, reading the screen. "That's a day."

"My running back?"

I showed her the display. "Your running back."

"Go, Eagles!"

Mom plays fantasy football with the teachers from her school. Practically all the players on her team are Philadelphia Eagles. Mom loves the Eagles. She knows that team the same way Red knows the NBA.

"Your hair is so brittle," she said, grabbing the sides of my head and turning it forward.

"This is where you tell me I'm not moisturizing my scalp enough."

She popped my ear.

"Ow!"

"Oh, please, Rip. That didn't hurt. If I wanted that to hurt, you would know."

I checked her phone again. "How much longer?" I asked.

"As long as it takes." She pulled the phone from my hand and placed it out of my reach. "If you're going to wear your hair like this, you're not leaving this house looking—"

"Tiki can ball," I interrupted.

"You working me now?" She leaned forward and turned my face her way.

"No."

"Out of nowhere you start talking about Tiki?"

"She's lefty. I've never played with a lefty before. That's going to mess with the other teams."

"How so?"

"Practically every kid goes right. On D, everyone gives kids the left without even realizing it. Tiki's going to blow by everyone."

"I'm glad to see you're giving her a chance."

"See how responsible and mature I am?"

"Now I know you're working me." She popped my ear again.

"Ow!" I ducked.

"Hold still." She pulled my head closer and stretched a lock above my neck. "You turned in all your forms?"

"Uh-huh."

"Yes?"

"Yes."

I looked over at the phone, but Mom pressed her hand to my cheek and faced me forward again.

"Do you think they'll ever change the cell-phone policy at RJE?" I asked.

"Not while you're a student there, unfortunately."

"It's stupid."

"It's an unfortunate situation. Don't get me started."

Actually, that's exactly what I wanted. We hadn't talked about the cell-phone policy in a while, and I needed to know she still felt the same way.

I was part of Operation Food Fight. Avery and Diego had convinced me to go along with it, and Mr. Acevedo had given us permission. Well, sort of. To be honest, I still didn't think it was the best idea, and I couldn't stand that Tiki was involved, but Operation Food Fight wasn't about Tiki. It was about the Lunch Bunch. We wanted the Lunch Bunch back.

"What those kids did last year, posting those pictures and videos, was awful," she said. "And once they started making all those comments, it took things to a whole other level. The parent reaction was completely understandable. But you don't throw the baby out with the bathwater."

I knew what that meant. Mom always used that expression when she talked about the district ban on cell phones and the end of the BYOD program in the elementary schools.

Mom's fingers moved to another lock. "You don't punish everyone when a few kids mess up," she said. "It sends the wrong message. And you definitely don't take away a valuable teaching tool. At my school, we have strict rules and guidelines for— Rip, I told you not to get me started!"

"Sorry."

Even though I wasn't.

"I feel bad for the next kids who pull a stunt like that." She chuckled. "And I feel even worse for their parents. That's not going to be a pleasant situation."

I swallowed.

"Honey, if you ever get caught doing something stupid, I hope you have the good sense to admit it, particularly if—"

"The schedule!" I turned from Mom's hands and tilted the computer screen. "No way!"

"Lean back, Rip. I'm almost done."

"I don't believe this," I said.

"What don't you believe?" She grabbed my collar and pulled me back.

"This has to be a mistake. We play Millwood again."

"Millwood? I thought you were playing all new teams."

"I thought so, too."

"It's still an eight-game season?"

"Uh-huh . . . I mean, yes." I read the schedule. "We open at home against Harrison a week from Tuesday. Then we play Bartlett, Fairlawn, Thorton Ridge, Walker, Yeager, and Cypress Village. Then Millwood. All new teams, except for Millwood."

"I wonder if that nut-job coach of theirs has something to do with this."

"We play them the last game of the season," I said.

"Coach Acevedo's going to love that."

"I guess we'll have to whup their butts again." I thumped my chest. "Just like we did at the end of last season."

Plots and Plans

To start the new week in Room 208, Mr. Acevedo kicked off a mini project called Where I Read. For the next three weeks, he wanted us to keep track of where we read. Then, in three weeks, we would conference.

"If you have any questions about this mini project," he said, "check the class page. I've posted all the expectations. I've also created a sample entry. You can use my template, or make a similar one on your own. Please keep track of your reading in your notebook. It's your responsibility to use our class page, especially if you don't understand something. I shouldn't have to tell you that anymore. We're in fifth grade now. I am not holding your hands."

I smacked my forehead. I couldn't stand it when Mr. Acevedo sounded *exactly* like Mom.

* * *

All week, lunch and recess turned into Operation Food Fight planning time. Diego took command. Like, seriously took command.

"We're running a professional operation here," he said while giving us copies of the lunch menu for every day in November. "We're thinking through every phase, we're planning out every phase, and we're not getting caught."

We decided to run three missions. The first two would be before Thanksgiving, and the third one would be right after the break. We were going to run a mission on a pizza day, but we decided we didn't need to since other kids were following Mr. Acevedo's suggestion. Miles was keeping track of how many kids bought pizza and how many kids brought lunch, and the OMG girls were standing at the garbage cans recording what was being thrown away—trays with full slices of pizza, trays with half-eaten pizza slices, trays with only pizza crust, trays with bread but no cheese, and trays with just cheese.

Not only did Diego make copies of the menus, but he also made full-color, detailed maps of the cafeteria. When I say detailed, I mean really detailed, right down to where the fire extinguishers were located and the fruit-and-vegetable nutrition charts were posted.

We all learned our roles, too. Since Avery had the camera, she was the team general. On mission days, she

would go through the lunch line twice—once with me, once with Diego. Red and Tiki were lookouts. Red would watch from the booth. Tiki would watch from one of three spots—seated at the second-grade tables, standing by the door to the gym, or waiting by the exit of the service area. It all depended on where the lunch-duty teachers were.

Then we practiced with the camera by the jungle gym. No lie, the whole time we did, I kept hearing Mom's voice in my head.

I feel bad for the next kids who pull a stunt like that. And I feel even worse for their parents. That's not going to be a pleasant situation.

But the thing is, no one noticed us. Even in plain sight on the playground, no one noticed the camera clamped to the back of Avery's chair.

Finally, we decided what we were going to do with the video evidence.

"We're not posting it online," I said jokingly, even though I wasn't joking.

"No kidding," Diego said.

Avery was going to edit the raw footage. After she did, we were all going to make a presentation like the one Avery and I made for our class project last month.

"We could take it to the news," Tiki said. "That would really blow the lid off this joint."

"Whatever, dude," Avery said. "We'll figure out who to share it with after it's all done, but not until. Agreed?"

We all agreed.

"Ooh, I love it when a plan comes together," Tiki said.

* * *

At basketball, Coach Acevedo kept on running us, and let me tell you, the conditioning was paying off. Yeah, we'd only been at it a week, but Clifton United was already in much better shape.

More stamina, more speed.

But since the first game was only a week away, Coach Acevedo was no longer all about running us until we dropped. We also focused on the basics—passing, rebounding, and setting picks. We worked on defense, too—learning the full-court press, practicing the trap, guarding the inbounds pass (under the basket and sideline), and switching. Coach Acevedo made sure everyone learned every position.

The more we practiced, the clearer it became how Coach Acevedo planned on using us in games. Well, at least it was clear to me. Keith and Dylan were definitely going to see the floor at the same time. Dylan was great at deflecting passes, forcing turnovers, and getting the rock to Keith where he could use it. Chris and Jeffrey were going to see a lot of time together, too. Chris brought out the best in Jeffrey, and when Maya played with them, the three held their own against any other three on the team.

I was going to be running the offense, bringing up the ball alongside Tiki.

Of course, at the end of every practice, Coach Acevedo had us shoot free throws.

"Clifton United takes free throws with tired arms and tired legs," he said over and over. "Winning teams make their free throws with tired arms and tired legs."

Starting

At the end of the last practice before the start of the season, Coach Acevedo gave out the uniforms. Just like he did last season. And just like last season, he gave them out when we were shooting our free throws.

"Rip and Red," he said, walking over with the large duffel bag slung over his shoulder. "Let me see that magic," he said to Red, who was at the line.

"Sure thing, Coach Acevedo," Red said.

He dropped the ball and trapped it underfoot soccer-style. He placed a finger over each ear and took several breaths. Then he picked up the ball with both hands, squared his shoulders, and stared at the front rim. He dribbled three quick times low to the ground, stood back up, and then rotated the ball until his fingers gripped it around the word SPALDING. He looked at the rim again, extended his arms, and shot the ball.

Swish!

"Our free-throw-shooting machine!" Coach Acevedo said. "You two want your uniforms?"

"Oh, yeah, Coach Acevedo." Red scooted over.

"They're the same ones as last season," Coach Acevedo said, reaching into his bag, "but I promise you, they're all clean." He handed Red his shirt.

Red hopped from foot to foot as he stared at the words CLIFTON UNITED written in gold cursive across the front. When he turned the shirt over, his mega-basketball smile widened. He ran his fingers over DANIELS written in block letters across the top and the number twenty-four beneath it.

I held out my fist. He gave me a pound.

"But wait, there's more," Coach Acevedo said, dipping his arm back into the duffel. "We have socks this season." He handed them to Red.

"Thanks, Coach Acevedo," he said. "Can I put them on now?"

Coach Acevedo laughed. "Absolutely." He reached back into the bag and flipped me my shirt.

Number thirty-two. Like last season. Like Rip Hamilton.

Then Coach Acevedo tossed me my matching navy socks.

"Thanks," I said.

"Take a walk with me, Rip." Coach Acevedo pointed

with his chin toward the corner of the gym. "Let's have a conversation."

"You're naming me assistant coach?"

"Not yet." He chuckled. "But I am very impressed with your leadership. You've set the example at every practice. Your energy and intensity are what we need from everyone this season."

"You know it."

"So let's talk strategy." He lifeguard-twirled his whistle. "We go thirteen deep, but that includes Red, so we really only go twelve." He glanced back at the court. "Emily and Max aren't going to get much playing time, so that brings us down to ten."

I leaned against the wall. "I figured that."

"So the plan is to go with two units, a first five and a second five."

"I like it."

"We're going to balance those two units so that we maintain the same level of pressure no matter who's on the court. Our second unit is going to run circles around every other team's bench." He snatched his whistle. "You're going to lead our second unit."

"The second unit?"

"Tiki's going to run the floor with the first unit, you're—"

"Tiki's starting?"

"Tiki's going to run the floor with the first unit," he said again. "You're going to run the floor with the second."

"So I'm . . . I'm not starting?"

"Tiki, Keith, Jason, Dylan, and Mehdi are the first five."

"How come—"

"We need you leading that second unit." He placed his hand on my shoulder.

I slid out from under it. "How can I not be starting?"

"Rip, I don't think you're hearing what I'm saying."

"Tiki just—"

"You're with Wil, Maya, Chris, and Jeffrey. I think that gives us our best shot at winning."

I gripped the socks with both hands. "Not playing me gives us our best shot at winning?"

"Who says you're not playing? You're leading our second unit."

"This is so not fair."

Coach Acevedo pulled back his hair. "I was hoping—"

"This is so not fair!" I threw down the socks and pointed to the court. "At every practice—"

"Rip," he said with an edge, "calm down."

"Does Tiki know?"

"I'm letting you know first because I wanted you to hear it from me. I wanted you—"

"Whatever, Coach." I kicked the floor. "I need to shoot my free throws." I walked away.

Benched and Floored

I sat on my bedroom floor and stared at my writer's notebook.

Where I Read   Saturday November 16

So far, I hadn't written a thing. I wasn't going to either.

I picked up the notebook and frisbeed it across my room. The open pages smacked the closet door. Then I grabbed the pen out of the pouch pocket of my hoodie and backhand-flung it in the same direction.

With both hands, I grabbed the locks above my neck and pulled.

How can I not be starting? How can I not be starting?

I tightened my lips and squinted. Then I squinted harder. Tears filled the corners of my eyes. The last time I cried was over the summer when Mom and I had a huge fight.

I looked up at the laptop on my workstation. It was still

open to Clifton United's site. This morning before practice, I'd been going over the diagrams and plays Coach had asked us to review.

How can Tiki be starting? How can Tiki be starting?

I let go of my hair and placed my hand atop the Sixers' logo on the throwback Iverson shirt sitting on the floor. I stared at my fingers, spread across the circle of small stars on the logo. The shirt was worn so thin I could see the blue number three on the back.

I never saw Iverson play live. I've only seen highlights of his crossover dribble. Right to left, left to right, breaking ankles, beating everyone.

Tiki had the killer crossover. She could beat everyone with her right to left. No one our age around here could guard that.

Tiki.

A tear slid from my eye. I rammed my elbow into the side of my mattress. Then I rammed it again.

Again, again, again . . .

Mission #1

Team Operation Food Fight stood in the alcove under the basket in the gym. In a moment, we'd head into the cafeteria for the first mission.

"We're bringing back the Lunch Bunch!" Avery said. She leaned back, popped a wheelie, and did a three-sixty.

"Oh, yeah." Red hopped.

"You sure you remember how to turn the camera on?" Diego asked Avery.

"Ask me that one more time, and I'm going to rip that penguin hat off your head and—"

"No need for violence." He held up his hands. "Just making sure."

"You know where to be?" Avery asked Tiki.

"Yeppers," she said. "I'm sitting with Mr. Noble's second graders."

Avery turned to Red. "You know what to do?"

"I know what to do, Avery Goodman."

She picked her book bag off the floor and held it out to me.

"Hook this to my chair. I would, but I don't want to accidentally touch the camera. Diego might explode."

Diego made an exploding sound and stumbled backward all the way to the foul line. Then he charged back over and rested his arm on my shoulder. "It's time to make some noise at RJE!"

"It is," I said.

"Are you nervous, Rip?" Tiki asked.

"No, Tiki, I'm not."

"You haven't said a word. I thought you—"

"I'm not nervous."

Furious was more like it.

For the rest of the weekend, I hadn't done much of anything. I'd spent most of yesterday by myself in my basement. This morning, when Red and I got to school, instead of going to Room 208, I waited in the bathroom until the other kids were allowed in.

"I'm so glad Ramadan is earlier this year," Tiki said.

"Where did that come from?" Diego asked.

"When I was little, Ramadan seemed to always fall in August." Tiki pressed her hands to her cheeks and shook her face. "That was the worst-ist-ist. You couldn't eat or drink during the day, and it was so hot."

"You fasted for Ramadan?" Diego asked.

"Kinda sorta." She snort-laughed. "Not like other people in my family. My pop says that not drinking water while fasting is the most essential part, but—"

"Why are we talking about this?" I asked.

"Why does Ramadan move?" Diego asked.

"It doesn't," Tiki said. "It's based on the lunar calendar, not the January-February-March-April calendar."

"How do you go a whole month without eating or drinking?" Diego asked. He checked the camera clamp on Avery's chair. "The only time I ever had to fast was before surgery. Now the only time I can go more than a few hours without food is when I'm sleeping!"

"You're allowed to eat and drink after sundown," Tiki said. "Do you know what everyone says at the end of Ramadan?"

I rolled my eyes. "I bet you're going to tell us."

"*Eid Muburak*," Tiki said. "That means 'blessed festival.'"

"Eid," Red said. "Like your last name, Takara Eid."

"Ding, ding, ding." She pointed her index fingers at Red and shifted her arms back and forth. "Everyone says my name. How awesome-sauce is that?"

"Why are we still talking about this?" I asked.

"Because this is just like an old baseball movie my pop loves," Tiki said. "In this one scene, all the players are standing around the pitcher's mound talking about jammed eyelids, live roosters, cursed gloves, and what to get someone for a wedding gift. Then the manager comes up and says candlesticks always make a nice gift."

We all stared.

"Okilee-dokilee." Tiki snort-laughed again. "I'm just trying to keep the team loose." She dropped her arms to her sides and shook them. "Like on the basketball court."

I chomped on my lip. If she said anything else about basketball, I was going to erupt like a volcano.

"When we're loose and relaxed," Tiki said, "we're more focused. We're on our game." She looked at me. "No one on Team Operation Food Fight should be scared or—"

"I'm not scared!" I snapped.

"I'm just—"

"Stop!" Avery interrupted. "You two are ridiculous." She pointed to the cafeteria. "Diego and I are going. Then me and Rip." She looked around the group. "Let's do this."

I checked Red. "You ready?"

"Ready as I'll ever be, Mason Irving."

"Someone's in a mood," Avery said. "What did Tiki do this time?"

"Nothing," I said.

We were on the lunch line approaching the entrance to the service area. As part of the plan, we were supposed to be in the middle of a conversation when we walked in, but Tiki was the last thing I wanted to be talking about.

I checked the cafeteria. The new first-grade teacher, Ms. Dunwoody, was eating lunch with her class and not paying much mind to the other students. Mr. Noble was standing near the exit to the service area grading papers. No, it wasn't exactly the best place for him to be, but I knew the only time he looked up was when someone came over.

I glanced at Tiki, sitting at the end of a second-grade table and facing the service area. The little kid next to her was practically in her lap. I so wanted that little booger to dump his beans and fruit all over her.

Red and Diego were at our booth. Diego had already gone through the line. I stared at his penguin hat. The eyes were too close together. They weren't just looking at me; they were looking *through* me. Were other eyes watching? All of a sudden, my thoughts jumped to Mom and Suzanne (Red's mom) and Principal Darling and . . .

"Stop!" Avery said.

I flinched. "What am I doing?"

"That freak-out face of yours," she said. "It's making me nervous." She rammed her chair into my leg.

"Ow," I said. "I can't stand when you do that."

"I can't stand when you do your freak-out face." She pointed. "Now focus, fart boy."

"Not funny."

She laughed. "I thought it was. Relax, dude." She motioned for me to go in. "Let's do this."

I entered the service area and grabbed a tray.

All four lunch ladies were there: one was serving the food, one was working the register, and the other two were in the back—one by the refrigerators, the other by the sinks.

I stepped to the counter. The lunch lady grabbed my tray and looked up. She motioned to the food with her gloved hand.

"I'll have the hamburger, please."

"Beans?" she grumbled.

Before I could say "No, thanks," she dumped a spoonful onto the tray. Then she grabbed some sweet potato fries, which looked like soggy shoelaces, and dropped them next to the beans.

I glanced back at Avery. The tiny red light behind her ear was on. The camera was recording everything.

Everything.

"Fresh fruit?" the lunch lady asked.

"Yes, please," I said.

She dunked her ladle into the metal basin, scooped out some syrup-soaked pears, and poured them onto my tray. Then she placed the tray on top of the counter and looked to Avery.

"Didn't you just come through a minute ago?" she growled.

I swallowed.

"Yeah," Avery said. "I didn't get anything, remember? I said I—"

"Hamburger or ham-and-cheese wrap?" the lunch lady interrupted.

"I'll take the wrap," Avery said. "And everything that comes with it. Thanks."

The lunch lady dropped the food-like substances onto her tray.

We worked our way down the line. When we reached the register, the lunch lady there motioned for me to swipe my card. Like the other lunch lady, she didn't greet me or say a word. Same with Avery. She just pointed her to the card reader and moved on to the next kid.

"Told you it would go fine, dude," Avery said as we exited the service area. She bumped the back of my leg with her chair. "Piece of cake."

"Piece of cake," I said, smiling and not minding the chair-knock.

* * *

"That was tight," Diego said, strumming the table and swinging his hat strings.

"It's all on video," Avery said. "The way they looked at us, the way they treated us, the food—everything."

The Operation Food Fight team was back at the booth.

"Sweet," Diego said. "Well done, crew."

Tiki shook her fingers like a cheerleader. "I just love it when a plan comes together."

Avery flicked the orange mush in the corner of her tray. "What is this?" she asked.

"I think that's the pineapple push-up," I said.

"No friggin' way," she said. "There's no way that's pineapple."

"I think it's a pear," I said.

"I think it's baby barf," Diego said.

"That's nasty," Red said, spinning his spork on the table. "If we do another That's Nasty project in Room 208, you have your topic, Avery Goodman."

I laughed. "Nice one, Red." I held out my fist.

He tapped it with his.

It was the first time I ever heard Red try to be funny or make a joke in front of anyone other than me.

"Yo, when we went through the line," Diego said, "the other lunch lady came up and dumped the corn out of this huge bucket into the serving tray. It looked like one giant yellow glob of alien boogers."

"Puke city!" Tiki said, sticking a finger into her mouth and making a throw-up face.

"Dude, you call this a wrap?" Avery swatted her ham-and-cheese.

"It looks like an unwrap!" Tiki snort-laughed.

"A flame-broiled hamburger on a whole wheat bun?" I said, jabbing my finger at my tray. "No way. That's a boiled burger on bread." I turned to Red again. "How did things go for you, Lookout?"

"Spindiddly," Tiki answered first.

I shot her a glare. "I was talking to Red."

"It went great, Mason Irving," Red said. "Ms. Dunwoody didn't notice a thing. Mr. Noble didn't notice a thing. Ms.—"

"BTW," Tiki interrupted, "*spindiddly* isn't my word. It's a word from a book I really, really like." She raised her fist. "I hereby declare our first mission a boom-boom-booming success!"

"I second that," Diego said, whipping around his hat strings.

"You know what would be amaze-balls?" Tiki said. "If

Clifton United's first game of the season tomorrow was a boom-boom-booming success, too!"

"Oh, yeah, Takara Eid," Red said.

"Don't you think so?" Tiki patted my shoulder.

I shrugged off her hand.

The Opener

"**Everyone should have** a few butterflies this afternoon," Coach Acevedo said. "That's how it should be before a season opener." He knelt in front of the five Clifton United starters, who sat on the chairs along the sidelines.

The rest of us stood around Coach Acevedo. I was directly behind him, standing next to Red with my arms folded tightly across my chest. Ever since he'd *benched* me the other day, I'd made it a point to make as little eye contact with him as I could, in the classroom and on the court. I stared at his earrings—silver hoops ran all the way up one ear, silver studs dotted his other.

"When that whistle blows and that ball goes up," he said, "we're going to outhustle those Harrison Hawks. In fact, we're going to run them out of our gym and right back onto their bus."

"Since they're Hawks, Coach," Chris said, smiling, "wouldn't the Harrison Hawks *fly* back to their bus?"

Coach Acevedo swatted him with his iPad. "That's the loose attitude I want from everyone."

"Wowz-o-wowzer!" Tiki said, patting her stomach. "My butterflies are going zooma-zooma-zoom!"

"I want you zooma-zooma-zooming on the court." Coach Acevedo held out his fist to Tiki.

She gave him a pound.

Tiki wore number three. Of course she wore number three. Iverson wore number three. She probably found out I loved Iverson and chose his number for that very reason.

"Everyone contributes," Coach Acevedo said, glancing around. He looked over his shoulder as if he was looking for me. "Whether you're on or off the floor, everyone contributes. Everyone."

I turned away. Across the gym, I spotted the kids from Room 208—Noah, Xander, Melissa, and the OMG girls, who were holding CLIFTON UNITED ROCKS signs.

"Before we take the floor," Coach Acevedo said, "we're starting a tradition." He stood and faced Red. "Number Twenty-Four."

"Yes, Coach Acevedo," Red said.

Coach soccer-style kicked up a basketball and flipped it to Red. "Go take a free throw."

"Right now?" Red pressed his earplugs, which softened the noise, and hopped from foot to foot.

"Right now. From now on, Blake Daniels takes a free throw before the start of every game. That's the Clifton United tradition we're starting today. Let's go."

Wearing his basketball smile, Red dribbled out to the far foul line.

I unwrapped my arms and lowered my clenched fists to my sides.

You got this, Red. You got this.

On the stage behind the basket, by the RESERVED FOR RJE FAMILY AND FRIENDS sign, the Clifton United parents stood and clapped. But only a few parents were here—Emily's dad, Mehdi's parents, and Dylan's father. I'd never seen Dylan's dad before, but I knew it was him because he also reminded me of Shaggy from *Scooby-Doo.*

Suzanne and Mom were here, too. I knew they were coming, but I hadn't told Mom that I wasn't starting and Tiki was. That was a mistake. She was going to make such a thing of it in the car ride home.

I checked the Hawks bench. All eyes on Red.

You got this, Red. You got this.

Red trapped the basketball under his left foot, pressed his earplugs, and took several breaths. Then he picked up the ball, squared his shoulders, and looked at the front rim. He dribbled three times—low, hard dribbles—and stood back up. Then he spun the ball until his fingers were right and looked at the rim again. He extended his arms and took the shot.

Underhanded.

Swish!

"Bam!" Red cheered.

He gobbled up the ball and charged back to the sideline. After everyone gave him high fives and pounds, Red and I started another tradition: our pregame, post-free-throw handshake.

"Roll left, roll right," we chanted. "Slap right, slap left." We jumped, bumped hips, and then when we landed . . .

"Boo-yah!"

* * *

"Shot!" the bench shouted.

Mehdi leaped for the rebound and fed Tiki on the wing. She caught the pass and, in one motion, put the ball on the floor with her left. As soon as her man picked her up at half-court, she dribbled behind her back—left to right—and blew by. At the three-point circle, she whipped the ball to Keith, streaking down the right.

Dribble. Shot. Score.

8–0, Clifton United.

"Match up, match up, match up!" Coach Acevedo called.

"Match up!" Red stood on his chair and waved a towel. "Match up!"

Harrison had no clue how to break our press. The time-out they called two minutes ago hadn't helped at all. We weren't bigger or better than them, but just like Coach Acevedo had said in the huddle before the game, we were running them out of the gym.

"Hands up, hands up, hands up!" Coach Acevedo waved.

"Hands up!" Red cheered.

I was cheering, too. I had to be a good teammate. But I wasn't going to stand on my chair and wave a towel.

Guarding the inbounds, Dylan waved his long arms and refused to allow the kid with the headband to get a good look. Finally, Headband threw an up-for-grabs pass between the foul line and the top of the key. Jason outjumped everyone and found Tiki by the elbow. She drove to the hoop and sank her second layup.

10–0.

"Let's go, second unit," Coach Acevedo said.

I checked the clock: 6:42 remained in the half. We led 16–5.

I always shift into basketball mode when I set foot on

the court, but when I took the floor with Wil, Maya, Chris, and Jeffrey, I didn't.

"Go get 'em, Mason Irving." Red waved his towel.

We were on defense. The Hawks were inbounding the ball under our basket. The only times they'd managed to score all game were when they didn't have to break the press.

Headband caught the inbound pass and drove past Wil for a bucket.

16–7.

"Let's go, Rip," Coach Acevedo said. "Be our floor leader."

I brought the ball up the court and passed to Maya on the left. She dribbled toward the corner and then sent the ball back to me.

"Way to be patient, Rip," Coach Acevedo said. "Reset our offense."

With my basketball eyes, I spotted Tiki. She was standing beside Coach and clapping like a kindergartner trying to clap as hard as she could.

I dribbled toward Wil. His man was overplaying him, so I picked up my dribble and faked a pass. The defender bit like I knew he would. Wil cut backdoor. He had a clear lane to the hoop. I fed him a perfect pass.

He doinked the layup.

I jumped up and down and grunted.

"Sprint back, sprint back, sprint back!" Coach Acevedo shouted.

I didn't. I pressed instead, and when Jeffrey and Wil saw me press, they pressed, too. Maya and Chris were the only ones back on defense. Harrison had a five-on-two fast break. Headband sank the layup.

16–9.

"Direct our team, Rip." Coach Acevedo pounded the back of his iPad. "Be our floor leader."

"Be our floor leader," Tiki said, still clapping hard.

Suddenly, I clicked into basketball mode. As I brought the ball up, I shook out my hair and waved Wil away. I needed space. As I approached the three-point circle, I began dribbling back and forth—right-left-right-left. The second I saw my man's knees buckle, I exploded by. At the elbow, I put up a jumper.

Front rim. Backboard. Basket.

18–9.

"Bam!" Red leaped off his chair.

"Press, press, press!" Coach Acevedo hopped up the sideline.

We pressed. Chris swarmed the man taking the ball out. The rest of us stuck to our men like flies on flypaper.

"Set picks! Set picks!" the Hawks coach shouted. "Move! Move without the ball!"

Tweet! Tweet!

“That’s a five-second violation.” The ref held up his hand. “Blue ball on the side.”

“Outstanding, Rip!” Coach Acevedo said. “That’s what we want to see.”

That’s what we want to see? Then play me more.

* * *

He didn’t play me more. He played me less.

In the second half, I stayed on the bench until the 6:17 mark. When I finally got in, we were already up 30–14.

“Close it out, Rip,” Coach Acevedo said as I trudged onto the floor.

I was playing garbage time. Yeah, we were going to win our first game, but I was playing garbage time.

This was garbage.

The Hot Seat

"Tiki is some ballplayer," Mom said, sliding into the driver's seat and pressing the ignition.

I leaned my head against the window and nodded once.

"How many points did she have? Ten? Fifteen?"

"I don't know."

Usually after my games, I'm nonstop talking—recapping hoops, passes, steals, moves, everything. And Mom listens, really listens. She even asks questions. But this afternoon, the last thing I wanted to do was talk about the game.

"I see you've been pulling on these." She touched the locks above my neck. "I really wish you wouldn't."

"Okay."

I didn't say anything else. Neither did she, and to be perfectly honest, the silence freaked me out a little. Yeah, the ride from RJE to our house wasn't much of a ride at all. If we made both lights, it was all of three minutes.

But it felt like three hours.

A block from our house, Mom stopped. Not pull-over stopped. She stopped in the middle of Key Place and put the car in Park.

"What are you doing?" I asked.

"You mind telling me what's going on?" She shifted in her seat and rested her elbow on the wheel.

"We're in the middle of the street." I pointed.

"Do you see any cars?" She clicked on the hazards. "That was the best I've ever seen any of your teams play, and you haven't said word one about it."

I pulled the old Nintendo DS from the door pocket.

"You're not going to say anything? Fine. I'll do the talking. Put the game away."

I dropped it back in and looked out the window.

"Don't you turn your back on me, Mason Irving!"

I flinched and faced her.

"You want to sit there and sulk or do whatever it is you're doing? Be my guest. But your eyes will be on me." She tapped the dashboard. "Watching Red out there today was such a joy. The way Coach Acevedo had him take that foul shot. That was wonderful. And seeing him on the sidelines cheering everyone. It's a beautiful thing that he's part of Clifton United." She paused. "Nothing to say?"

No.

"Fine." Mom shook her head. "I will tell you, I was a little surprised to see you press like that. I didn't like it when Millwood pressed last season, but I think that may have had more to do with that coach of theirs."

I still said nothing.

She leaned in. "Honey, why didn't you tell me you weren't starting?" she said in a softer tone.

I let out a puff.

"Obviously you have a problem with coming off the bench. Not exactly a team-first attitude, Rip."

"My attitude is fine." I finally spoke. "I played hard. I cheered on my teammates."

"Honey, you're right." She shook her head again. "You didn't do anything wrong."

She turned off the hazards and started to drive.

"Life is about playing the cards you're dealt, Rip," she said.

I leaned my head against the window again and closed my eyes.

The Bench Mob

In the layup lines before the start of our second game, Clifton United was looking good and looking loose. So I tried to look good and loose, too.

"Go, Max!" everyone sang as he drove to the basket. "Go, Max!"

Then when the ball went through the rim . . .

"Whoosh!"

We chanted the same thing for everyone.

"Go, Red! Go, Red!"

Red dribbled to the hoop and put up his layup.

"Whoosh!"

As Red ran past on his way to the end of the rebound line, I reached out and rubbed his head. He ducked away, but I still got in a good rub. It was the first time I'd ever tried that.

Red mega-basketball smiled.

I looked back toward the stage. Only Mehdi's dad and

Chris Collins's parents were here today. Suzanne had to work nights the rest of the week, and Mom had an after-school meeting.

Not many kids from class showed either. Only Melissa and Xander.

Fine by me. I didn't need all of Room 208 watching Tiki start and me sit.

* * *

Coach Acevedo gave his pregame talk, Red sank his traditional free throw, and the Clifton United first unit took the floor against the Bartlett Bulldogs.

On the sidelines, I decided to take a different approach. Instead of standing with Red and Max, who were on their chairs and waving towels even before the tip, I grabbed the seat next to Coach Acevedo. It would keep me on his radar. He'd put me in sooner.

Once again, we jumped out to an early lead. Like the Hawks, the Bulldogs had no idea what to make of our press. Six minutes in, we were already up 12–4, and when Coach Acevedo signaled for a time-out, I thought for sure he was bringing in the second unit.

"Outstanding!" he said to the first unit. "I love to be dazzled, and you are dazzling me." He turned to Tiki. "Way to be the floor leader out there. Keep it going." He motioned to the court. "That's all I wanted to say. Same five, let the dazzling continue."

So much for being on his radar.

I walked to the end of the bench and stopped in front of Max and Red, who were back on their chairs and twirling their towels. I would cheer for my teammates. Of course I would, but I wasn't about to go wild like they were.

I didn't see the floor until there were five minutes left in the half. By then, the game was a done deal. We were already up by sixteen. First-half garbage time.

"Let's go, second unit." Coach Acevedo waved us up.

Wil, Maya, Chris, Jeffrey, and I headed onto the court.

"Let's go, Bench Mob." Tiki kindergarten-clapped as she bounded off.

"Bench Mob!" Coach Acevedo said, smiling. "Nice! I like that." He pointed the second team in. "Let's go, Bench Mob!"

"Let's go, Bench Mob." Red waved his towel.

I grabbed the locks above my neck. Fart-boy Rip was now head of the Bench Mob.

"Way to be our floor leader, Tiki," Coach Acevedo said. "Way to be our Rookie of the Year."

I kicked at the court.

Mission #2

Team Operation Food Fight was in position: Red was sitting at the booth, Tiki was standing by the middle garbage cans, Diego was at the back of the line, and Avery and I were a couple kids away from the entrance to the service area.

Mission two was under way.

"This line is taking forever," Avery said.

"You'd think it would move faster because there's no choice today," I said.

"Exactly. Everyone's getting the same friggin' meal. These lunch ladies have no idea what they're doing."

Today was the Thanksgiving lunch—honey-roasted turkey, golden yams, seasoned mashed potatoes, traditional holiday stuffing, and pumpkin pie. Whether or not the foods that ended up on our trays resembled anything close to those items remained to be seen.

I checked the lunch-duty teachers. Ms. Dunwoody sat

with her first graders, just like she had during the first mission. I still didn't know the name of the teacher by the door to the gym. She taught third grade. She never spoke to the fifth graders. We thought she was scared of us.

I stepped into the service area. "We need to be talking," I said.

"What do you want to talk about?" Avery asked.

"I don't know."

"Fine." She knocked my leg with her armrest. "We'll talk about the lunch ladies. I made up names for them."

"What?"

"I made up nicknames for the lunch ladies." Avery nodded to the lunch lady serving the food. "That's Donatella."

"Not here," I said through my teeth.

"For the last mission," she said, "she wore a purple—"

"Not here," I said, cutting her off.

"Relax, dude. We're just talking. Last time, she wore a purple sweatshirt under her uniform. I noticed it as I was going through the footage. The purple reminded me of Donatello. Like Ninja Turtle Donatello. So I call her Donatella." She pointed to the lunch lady by the register. "She's Bunion."

"Stop, Avery." I was next in line. "Talk about something else."

"Fine. Let's talk about the Bench Mob."

"How do you know about that?"

"Dude, I'm a Clifton United fan." She tapped the inside of her wrist and smiled. "I have my finger on the pulse of the team."

I let out a puff.

"You're 2–0," she said. "You should be happy."

"I am happy," I muttered.

"Tiki's a beast out there. Fifteen points the first game, twelve points yesterday. Did you have any idea she was this good?"

"The other teams don't know about our press yet. We'll see what happens when word gets out."

"They don't know about Tiki!"

I looked from Avery to the lunch lady and back to Avery. "Does anyone else know you came up with these nick-names?"

"Not yet."

The lunch lady tapped her plastic spoon against the side of the Plexiglas. "What's it going to be, young man?" she asked.

"I think I'll—"

"I'll make it easy for you," she cut me off.

She dropped a clump of mashed potatoes into one corner of the tray and a scoop of stuffing into another. She then plopped some yams beside the stuffing.

"Thank you," I said. I grabbed my prewrapped slice of pumpkin pie and headed for the register line.

"Donatella was pleasant," Avery said, rolling up next to me. "Let's see how Bunion is."

I checked the lunch lady by the register. "Why do you call her that?"

"Because she wears her hair up in a bun."

I motioned to the two lunch ladies in the back. "What are their names?"

"Over by the sink, we have Tarantula. Something about the way she moves her arms makes me think of one. And over by the fridge, we have Ratio, which I do admit is a lame name." She snapped her fingers. "Maybe if I go behind the counter and get a closer look at her, I'll come up with a better one."

"Not funny, Avery."

"We'll have footage from all different angles." She wheeled past me. "We'll even have shots of the inside of the refrigerator."

"Avery, wait!"

She rolled up to Bunion, hockey-stopped beside her, and turned for the opening into the kitchen . . .

. . . and nearly ran into Principal Darling.

"Slow down, Speed Racer!" Principal Darling said. She grabbed both armrests. "You almost ran me down."

"That was close!" Avery said.

"A little too close, Avery." Principal Darling shook her head. "Obey the traffic laws. No accidents, please."

"No accidents," Avery said.

Tarantula handed Principal Darling an already prepared holiday meal, and Principal Darling headed off.

"Yikes," Avery said, grinning.

I grabbed the back of my neck and squeezed. "I'm buggin' out over here."

"Relax, dude."

"If they'd caught you back there—"

"I would've talked my way out of it in a second." She bumped my leg again. "I'm the girl in the wheelchair, remember?"

"Don't go back there, Avery." I brushed the locks from my forehead. "It's too risky."

"Time to go through the line with Diego."

"Don't go back there." I stepped into her path. "Promise me you won't when you go through with Diego."

She nodded.

"No, promise me you won't. You have to say it."

"I promise I won't go back there when I go through with Diego."

Where I Read

I looked back at the hoop above my closet and shifted my already extended arm a little to the right. I rolled the Nerf out to my fingertips and tap-turned the ball until the seam was in line with my knuckles. Then I took the no-look, over-the-shoulder, from-halfway-across-my-bedroom bank shot.

Swish.

I scooped up the ball and plopped back down in front of my notebook.

"Keep up with your Where I Read work this weekend," Mr. Acevedo had said at CC on Friday. "It's the only homework you're getting from me, and I really don't even consider it homework. It's going to help us down the road."

I didn't keep up with it. Yeah, I read over the weekend. I always read. But I didn't write down where I did the reading. I saved that part until Sunday night. Mom said I couldn't watch football or have the Wi-Fi password until I did it.

I grabbed my purple teddy from my bed and popped to my feet. With my bare toes, I gripped the Nerf and flipped it up. I caught it with my left hand and tossed it right back into the air, and then, using the bear's belly, I hit the ball toward the hoop.

Swish.

"Bang!"

I never missed the purple teddy belly shot.

I scrambled after the ball and then dove back to my notebook.

Basement
Car
Kitchen table
Bed
Hood

"Rip to his feet," I muttered as I jumped up again. "He sizes up his man. Looks for an opening. He jukes right, crosses to his left, drives down the lane, the running one-hander with his left . . .

". . . Boo-yah!"

Road Test

Before the start of our first away game at Fairlawn, Coach Acevedo flipped the ball to Red. "Go do your thing," he said.

Like Red did at our first two home games, he dribbled out to the foul line and took his underhanded free throw.

Swish.

"Bam!" Red pinched his number twenty-four. "Three for three!"

He scooped up the ball and raced back to the bench. I double high-fived him first, and then we rolled our arms right into our handshake.

"Boo-yah!" we shouted as we landed.

"Three for three." Red hopped from foot to foot as he slapped hands and gave pounds all around. "I made the foul shot before the game against Harrison. I made the foul shot before the game against Bartlett. I made the foul shot before the game against Fairlawn."

"Now Clifton United needs to make it three for three," I said.

"Oh, yeah, Mason Irving. Oh, yeah."

I rubbed Red's hair. Just like I did the other day. And like the other day, I got in a good rub before he ducked.

He smiled the whole time.

I checked the gym. The court was our real opponent today. It was middle school–sized, much bigger than the one we were used to practicing and playing on at RJE. We would have to cover a lot more ground on our press.

I needed to be out there. The Gnat needed to be out there playing suffocating defense. Coach Acevedo had to know that. He had to play me. If he didn't play me today . . .

"Let's circle up," Coach Acevedo said. "Time for our road test." He waited until everyone was standing on the word *VISITORS* in front of our bench. "We all know the deal. We have back-to-back games this week before the Thanksgiving break, but we take these games one at a time."

"One game at a time, one possession at a time," Tiki said.

"Exactly," Coach Acevedo said. "That's how we're going to beat these guys."

I looked over at the Fairlawn bench.

The players all stood around the word *FALCONS* written in red on the gym floor. The red matched the trim, letters, and numbers on their uniforms, full uniforms—jerseys, shorts, and socks. A group of Fairlawn parents sat directly behind the bench. One mom was wrapping orange slices in paper towels.

We only had two fans today. Mehdi's dad, of course. And Chris's mom.

"We're playing on a big court," Coach Acevedo said, "but that's going to affect them more than it affects us. We're ready for this. This is where all our conditioning pays dividends, and if you don't know what *dividends* means, look it up when you get home."

I'm pretty sure I knew what *dividends* meant, but at the moment, I didn't care.

"It's time for Clifton United's press-tacular press!" Tiki raised an arm and pushed her hip out to the side.

"Press-tacular!" Coach Acevedo smiled. "I like that." He patted his iPad. "Even if they're ready for our press, they've never had to face it in a real game. That means they're reacting to us. That means we're setting the tone. We come out strong. We beat them early."

I clenched my fists. I needed to be out there. Clifton United needed me out there.

* * *

"Tiki with the smothering defense," I play-by-played. "She's got her man tied up . . . and the ball's loose. It's picked up by another Falcon player . . . Oh, stolen by Dylan. Dylan's got the ball. He hands off to—"

Tweet! Tweet!

"We've got a reach-in foul on number eleven on red," the ref called. He patted his arm where the Falcon player had smacked Dylan. "Blue ball on the side."

I didn't want to do the play-by-play, but Red insisted,

and I knew he wouldn't stop bugging me until I did. Once I started, Clifton United went on a run, so I couldn't stop.

"Six minutes gone and Clifton United leads 7–4. What once was a four-point deficit is now a three-point lead. That press of theirs is really causing problems for the Falcons. Keith is set for the inbounds on the near side . . ."

"Ref, let me get a time-out," Coach Acevedo said.

Tweet! Tweet!

"Time-out, blue!" the ref announced.

"Let's go, Bench Mob," Coach Acevedo said. He pointed my way. "We're switching things up."

I bolted over. Not what I was expecting. Not in a gazillion years. But I was ready. I was so ready.

"Let's do this, Bench Mob!" Keith topped fists with Maya.

"This is all you, Rip." Dylan forearmed my chest.

I pumped both fists and pivoted into Tiki.

She gave me double pounds.

I pulled back my hands. I didn't mean to give her pounds.

"I don't want you to like me just because I'm good at basketball," Tiki said.

"What?"

"I don't want you to start liking me because of

basketball." She blew a bubble. "Some kids are like that, you know."

"No." I swallowed.

"Yes." She snort-laughed. "Zwibble." She tapped my wrist.

I yanked it away.

"I just gave you my good-luck touch," she said. "I touched you with my fave-a-fave word."

"You're so weird, Tiki."

Coach Acevedo rapped his iPad. "Let's go, Bench Mob," he said. "Same intensity, same energy. No letdown."

"No letdown, Mason Irving." Red held out his fist.

"Letdown?" I gave him a hard pound and spun to my teammates. "The Bench Mob is about to show the first unit how it's done!"

* * *

I took the inbounds from Maya and lofted a pass to Chris down low. He was already facing the basket when he caught the ball. He dropped the easy deuce.

9–4.

The Falcons inbounded the ball to my man. Well, they tried to. It never reached him. I leaped around him, caught the rock, and before landing, touch-passed the ball back to Chris. Another easy deuce.

11–4.

"Way to set the tone, Rip." Coach Acevedo clapped.

"Bench Mob!" cheered Clifton United from the sidelines. "Bench Mob!"

The inbounds went to my man again. This time, he caught it, but as soon as he did, I stripped it away. The ball bounced off his shin and out of bounds.

Tweet! Tweet!

The ref patted his leg and pointed. "Off red, blue ball!"

I brushed the locks off my forehead and checked the bench. Red, Max, Emily, Keith, Jason, Dylan, Mehdi, and Tiki were all standing and cheering.

Maya passed the ball in to me. I dribbled toward the top of the key and sized up my man. For less than a nanosecond, his eyes danced. I broke to the hoop with my bedroom move. I dribbled right, crossed to my left, drove down the lane, and put up a running one-hander.

Swish!

13–4.

"Boo-yah!" I hammer-fisted the air.

Time-out, Fairlawn.

* * *

The Bench Mob played the rest of the half. Then we started the second half. When the first unit finally came back in with nine minutes to go, Clifton United led 30–13.

Garbage time.

I finished with eight points, five steals, five assists, and two rebounds.

Clifton United was 3–0.

Perked Up

"My shot was on today," I said.

"Four for five from the floor, Mason Irving," Red said, rotating his finger around the cup holder in the middle armrest. "A jumper from the corner, a jumper from the elbow, a layup, and a layup."

We were in the backseat of my mom's car. I was on the driver's side, Red the passenger's side. Like we always sat. Heading home from ball, we'd stopped at Perky's—the overpriced coffee shop Mom always complains about, but goes to anyway—and while she dipped inside, we waited in the car.

"Did you see that crossover I had?" I asked.

"That was awesome!"

"I looked like Iverson." I waved my hands back and forth in front of my knees like I was dribbling. "That kid I blew by is still looking for his tighty-whities."

Red laughed. "Your crossover's as good as Takara Eid's."

I gave him a look. "Why'd you bring her up?"

"Takara Eid's on Clifton United, Mason Irving."

I let out a puff. Through the storefront windows, I could see Mom standing in front of the glass counter with all the muffins and doughnuts. Mom almost never went to Perky's in the evening, but she said she needed coffee tonight if she had any hopes of finishing the paperwork she wanted to get out of the way before Thanksgiving weekend.

"When was the last time you had coffee?" I asked.

"I don't like coffee," Red said. "Do you?"

"Only with tons of sugar." I'd taken off my sneakers and socks when we got in the car, and with my bare toes, I opened and closed the air vents. "Whenever I drink it, my mom always says, 'Have some coffee with your sugar.'"

"Have some coffee with your sugar," Red said. "That's a good one, Mason Irving."

Inside, Mom was talking to Dana. Dana was the other reason we'd stop at Perky's. She was an assistant principal at a different school in my mom's district. She liked to bring her laptop and work at the back tables at Perky's. She called it her second office. Dana and Mom had been hanging out a lot these past few weeks.

"Did you see my touch pass to Chris?" I said. "And what about that dime to Maya to start the second half?"

"What about that steal you had when you knocked the ball off that kid's leg?"

"Clifton United's defense was suffocating!" I pounded the armrest. "Suffocating. They couldn't even get the ball in." I faced Red. "Coach Acevedo's definitely going to play me more, right, Red?"

"Definitely, Mason Irving."

Yeah, Coach Acevedo had to play me more. He had to.

Odd Man Out

Twenty-two hours and fifteen minutes later . . .

I couldn't wait to set foot on the floor at Thorton Ridge Elementary. After the *clinic* I put on yesterday at Fairlawn, I was itching to get right back on the court and do it all over again.

What a court!

This was no ordinary elementary school gym. Thorton Ridge had a full athletic center, a separate building behind the school. The basketball court had parquet floors, real benches, four rows of bleachers on each side, and an LED scoreboard with advertisements.

Because of the holiday, we were missing three key players, the twins and Dylan. Two out of our five starters weren't here. Other members of Clifton United would need to step in and step up.

Like me.

* * *

"Let's circle up," Coach Acevedo said.

Red and I were already in front of our bench waiting for the pregame meeting.

"As you can see," Coach Acevedo said, once everyone had jogged over, "we're a little shorthanded. We can't just swap the starters for the Bench Mob. So here's what we're going to do. Chris and Max, you're with the first five today."

"What?" I blurted.

Everyone looked my way, everyone except Coach Acevedo.

"Chris and Max," he said, "you're starting with Keith, Mehdi, and Tiki."

"Max is starting?" I said.

"Max is starting," Coach Acevedo repeated.

"After yesterday, how can you sit me?"

Coach Acevedo looked at me.

I looked away.

* * *

I didn't play the first half. I sat and watched the whole time. I didn't cheer. Not at all. A few times, Red tried to get me to stand up and join him, Wil, and Maya, but I wasn't having it.

Chris led the way. He played even better than he had

yesterday. On offense, he controlled the boards, grabbing four rebounds. On defense, he forced three turnovers. As for Max, I have to say, he did much better than I thought he would. Tiki made sure he knew where to be on offense. He didn't score, but he did grab an offensive rebound. He also made a couple sweet passes.

* * *

"Let's keep playing Clifton United basketball," Coach Acevedo said as the starting five got set to take the floor for the second half. He motioned to the scoreboard. "We've got a nice twelve-point cushion. Let's keep playing this one possession at a time."

The first time Tiki brought the ball up the court, Thorton Ridge double-teamed Chris. So she passed to a wide-open Max, who drove to the hoop for his first basket of the season.

"Max Stevens!" Red, Maya, and Wil chanted and clapped. "Max Stevens!"

Then, believe it or not, Max stole the inbounds pass and drove to the hoop for another layup!

"MVP!" Red, Maya, and Wil pounded the floor. "MVP!"

Coach Acevedo finally put me in with seven minutes left, but only because Tiki had a cut on her arm. By that point, we were up by twenty.

I was done.

"Rip, a word, please," Coach Acevedo said after the game.

He'd just finished speaking to the team and had sent everyone else to the bus.

"What's our record?" he asked.

"What?"

"Clifton United." He stepped closer. "What's our record?"

With my thumb and index finger, I twisted a lock near my forehead at its root. "4–0."

"4–0," he said. "Pretty good, right?"

I shrugged.

"No?" Coach Acevedo made a face.

I let out a puff.

"We've found a formula that works," he said. "We can't argue with success."

Happy Writing Day

"It's a pretty sparse crowd here in Room 208 this morning," Mr. Acevedo said at CC the next day. "I expected that the day before the long weekend."

I checked the meeting area. There were only fifteen kids. The last time we had so few kids was in third grade, when the stomach bug that made you feel like you were going to explode from both ends was going around.

I wished that bug on Mr. Acevedo.

He sat on the floor, leaning against the couch with both arms stretched out on the cushions. Since there were only fifteen of us, everyone was on the carpet or a beanbag.

"A lot of districts are off today," Mr. Acevedo said. He nodded to me. "Does your mom have school?"

I shook my head.

"I know some districts have off all week," Mr. Acevedo said. "So here's what we're going to do today." He patted the couch cushions. "Happy Writing Day!"

"We're doing writing today?" Piper asked.

"We are," Mr. Acevedo said. "Just because we're missing a few people doesn't mean we can't be productive and creative. I'll be writing, too."

"What's the topic, Mr. A.?" Zachary asked.

"A perfectly timed question." Mr. Acevedo tightened an earring. *"El aburrimiento se cura con curiosidad. La curiosidad no se cura con nada."*

"The cure for boredom is curiosity," Zachary translated. "There is no cure for curiosity."

"Exactly." Mr. Acevedo strummed the carpet. "*Mi abuela* used to say that all the time. When it comes to curiosity, it's my favorite expression, but *mi abuela* didn't come up with that one. I believe Dorothy Parker did."

"And if you don't know who Dorothy Parker is," Attie said jokingly, "look it up."

"Not a bad suggestion." Mr. Acevedo smiled. "So that's our topic for today. Curiosity. What are you curious about? That's what I want you to write about. Interpret that any way you wish."

I grabbed the back of my neck and squeezed.

"Curiosity is permitted," he said.

"Not everywhere," Attie called out.

"Sadly, no, it isn't." Mr. Acevedo drew a circle in the air with his finger. "But in Room 208, it is. In here, curiosity is encouraged."

"In some places," Attie said, "they don't like when you ask questions."

"Why can't you ask questions?" Piper asked.

"Questions deserve answers," Mr. Acevedo said. "But sometimes the answers make people uncomfortable, and people don't like being uncomfortable. I think people *need* to feel uncomfortable sometimes." He looked my way. "It forces them to think, forces them to reflect." He rapped his knees. "Let's get poppin'."

Journal Entry, 11/27

- I'm curious why some people say Thanksgivings late this year. Its not late. Its the forth Thursday of November likes every year. Its not the fifth Thursday of November because that would make it December.

- I'm curious why everyone is always afraid of the principal. They always say they your friend, but everyone is always still afraid of them a little bit not matter what. That's how it is for me.

- I'm curious about why you asked me our record after the game?

- I'm curious why some boys are embbarrassed by their stuffed animals. That's not how it is for me.

- I'm curious why everyone likes stuffing on Thanksgiving. Stuffing you're face untill you want to puke your guts out. Stuffing you're face until you need to explode out of your mouth and your butt!!

- I'm curious why you didn't play me. I should've played. I should've started. I earned it. You were wrong.

Swooping and Hooping

"Bam!" Red shouted as his behind-the-back shot from atop the scoreboard sailed through the net.

He sprang out of his gaming chair, hopped in front of the television, and hammer-fisted the air like I do.

I laughed. "Are you mocking me, Blake Daniels?"

He pinched his thumb and index finger. "I crush you," he said, speaking in a weird accent. "I crush you like an ant, Mason Irving."

We were in my basement playing Horse on Xbox. We hadn't been playing as much lately because of basketball, but we were more than making up for it today.

"H-O-R for Allen Iverson," Red said, "and H for Walt 'Clyde' Frazier."

I slid off the couch onto the floor. "I can read the scoreboard."

"You're boring me, Mason Irving." Red fell back into his chair. "I'm slicing and dicing, and you're bumbling and stumbling."

"Keep talking, Red. Keep talking."

Horse is the only video game Red can really play, but let me tell you, he can play. I used to be able to beat him, but not anymore.

He knows it, too.

We only play the Legends version. I'm always Iverson, and Red's a different player every time. Today, he was Walt "Clyde" Frazier, and he was not only telling me all about him, but also rhyming like Frazier does when he calls NBA games on TV.

"Walt 'Clyde' Frazier was a seven-time all-star," Red said. "Walt 'Clyde' Frazier was a seven-time, first-team NBA defensive player. Spinning and winning."

I moved Iverson to atop the scoreboard and took the behind-the-back shot. I sank it.

"Time for some bounding and astounding," Red said.

"You hungry?" I sat up.

"After yesterday, I don't think I'll ever eat again."

"You say that every year after Thanksgiving."

"This year I mean it, Mason Irving."

"I'm still full, too." I lifted up the front of my hoodie, pushed out my belly, and patted my stomach. "But I can always eat. What was the best thing they served?"

"Everything." Red rocked his chair.

Red and Suzanne always spent Thanksgiving with Suzanne's coworkers. Some of the nurses who lived together by the hospital had an all-day open house. That way, everyone who had to work on Thanksgiving could still celebrate it.

"You have to pick one food," I said.

"The macaroni and cheese!"

I grabbed the back of his chair and rocked it. "You'd better not get explosive macaroni-and-cheese trots in my basement!"

"If you're trying to distract me, it's not working, Mason Irving." He positioned Frazier on top of the backboard at the far end of the court. "In game seven of the 1970 NBA Finals, Walt 'Clyde' Frazier scored thirty-six points and had nineteen rebounds as the New York Knicks defeated the Los Angeles Lakers 113–99. But most people remember that game because Willis Reed—"

"Take your shot!"

He took another behind-the-back shot. It went in.

"Bam!" Red said. "Take that!"

"That was so lucky!"

"All skill, Mason Irving! Swooping and hooping." He turned around. "What was your favorite food?"

"Dana made this pepper dish that was off the hook, and Rhonda and Courtney made this turkey-sausage stuffing that was crazy."

"Who are Rhonda and Courtney?"

"My mom's friends. You've been to their house."

"The ones with the dogs?" Red said. "Edith and Archie?"

"Only Edith now. I played with her the whole time."

I set Iverson for a behind-the-back shot. It didn't even come close to reaching the backboard.

"H-O-R-S for Iverson," Red said. "H for Walt 'Clyde' Frazier. Looks like Mason Irving is losing again."

"Keep it up." I kicked at his chair. "You can go find another place to stay tonight."

Suzanne was working the rest of the weekend so that she could have off Christmas Eve and Christmas Day. Red was staying here. He always spent the Friday after Thanksgiving with me, but this was the first time he was staying over.

"Do you think Takara Eid's family celebrated Thanksgiving?" Red asked.

"How should I know?" I said. "Why did you have to bring her up?"

Red walked Frazier to the top row of the arena at the far end of the court. "Takara Eid's strategy for the Clifton United is working."

"It's not her strategy."

"Clifton United is undefeated." He peeked back. "Just like me."

"Listen to you, talking trash."

"Talking the truth, Mason Irving."

He heaved the shot. It went in.

"Bam!" He jumped in front of the television and raised his arms. "H-O-R-S-E. Don't even bother taking the shot.

You have no shot. Game over. Shaking and baking, out-muscling and outhustling."

I dropped my controller and threw a pillow at his legs.

He kneed it away. Then, suddenly, Red dove on top of me, grabbed the back of my shirt, and pulled it over my head.

To be perfectly honest, I didn't know whether to laugh or fight back. Red and I never wrestled. Never. I play-fight and wrestle with Xander, Noah, and Declan all the time, but not Red.

This was the first time he'd ever done this.

"Who's your daddy now, Mason Irving?" he said, sitting on my chest and holding my arms against the carpet.

"You're going to pay for this."

"Clifton United is a team," Red said, basketball-smiling. "Everyone contributes."

I tried to squirm out, but he had me pinned tight.

"Clifton United needs you, Mason Irving."

I freed my arm. "I need a rematch." I rolled out from under him.

"Oh, yeah, Mason Irving! Walt 'Clyde' Frazier will take down Allen Iverson one more time."

Good

I walked into Room 208 and straight up to Mr. Acevedo.

"Welcome back, Rip," he said. "How was the holiday?"

I held out my fist.

He gave me a pound. "We good?"

"We're good."

Mr. Acevedo smiled. "A few days away does a body good."

I flung my bag onto my table. It slid off and onto the floor. I looked at Mr. Acevedo and shrugged.

Then Red and I headed for the cafeteria.

Pushing the Envelope

I stood on a table in the cafeteria and shot the tinfoil ball.

"Off," I said the moment it left my fingers. "I'm rusty from the weekend." I clapped to Red. "Send that back."

Red glanced at the door to the service area and scampered after the tinfoil. "Last one, Mason Irving," he said nervously. He scooped it up, tossed it my way, and raced back next to the garbage can.

Red was getting my misses. I was standing much closer than usual, but I'd still missed my first three. I never missed four in a row.

"We should go, Rip." He held his fists next to his cheeks. "We're pushing the envelope too far."

"Pushing the envelope? Since when do you say that?"

"Mr. Acevedo said it."

"I know he did." I smiled. "I didn't know you did."

"We should go," Red said again.

"Irving squares his shoulders," I announced. "He fires from long distance . . ."

Once again, I knew it was off the second the tinfoil left my hand. I jumped off the table and charged after it.

"We should go," Red said, turtling his neck and pressing his elbows to his sides.

"One last shot." I gobbled up the ball, sidestepped to the kitchen entrance, and peeked in.

"Rip, no. What are you doing?"

"You know what Avery calls the lunch lady who moves her arms like this?" I shook my arms above my head and then waved them in different directions. "Tarantula."

He slid his hands behind his neck and squeezed his head with his arms.

"You know what she calls the one who wears her hair up? Bunion." I tossed the tinfoil behind my back with my right hand and caught it with my left. "On the last mission, she—"

"Stop." Red squinched his face tight, wrinkling his eyes, nose, and forehead. "Stop."

Old-man face. I didn't like Red's old-man face.

"Stop, stop, stop," he said.

I stopped. I didn't take the one last shot.

Mission #3

I looked over at Red sitting in the booth. He was supposed to be on lookout, but he had his head down, and his knees were bouncing against the underside of the table.

That's why Diego was sitting across from him scoping out the cafeteria.

I'd pushed the envelope too far during tinfoil basketball. I'd thought after the way we'd joked around and hung out all weekend—and even wrestled for the first time ever—that he could handle it. But I was wrong. Seriously wrong. All morning in Room 208, Red pinky-thumb-tapped his legs and wouldn't say a word. When Ms. Yvonne pushed in to work with him, he stayed silent. At one point he was rocking back and forth so hard, she had to hold him by the shoulders. Finally, she took him to her room. I couldn't remember the last time Red was pulled out of class.

I let out a puff. Avery and I were only a couple steps

from the service area, and thinking about Red was going to make me shake and sweat and bug. I needed to focus on the mission. This was our last chance to get what we needed to help bring back the Lunch Bunch.

"Remember the time the Lunch Bunch came dressed as the Power Rangers for Halloween?" I said to Avery.

"Remember when Ms. Audrey sang the song from *Aladdin* at the talent show?"

"She wore the genie costume," I said.

With my basketball eyes, I checked the lunch-duty teachers. Ms. Shore, whom we had in first grade, was talking with a group of boys. Ms. Harper, a new teacher whose name I just learned, was standing with Mr. Goldberg, the school custodian. They were right behind Tiki, who was on lookout near the garbage cans.

"When I get home this afternoon," Avery said, "I'll edit and label today's footage. Then we'll start making the presentation."

"We're going to get the Lunch Bunch back."

"Dude, I'm pumped." She pounded her armrests. "Bunion, Ratio, Tarantula, Donatella—your days are numbered. You're about to get what you deserve. Today's the day we seal the deal."

I glanced at the menu scribbled on the board next to the door.

"Wait here," Avery said.

"Where are you going?"

She wheeled into the service area, toward the opening that led to the back. "We need shots from angles—"

"Avery, no."

"Dude, relax. We still don't have any clean shots of the storage area and the sinks. It'll take two seconds."

"No, it won't." I glanced at Donatella and Tarantula standing by the refrigerator. "They're right there."

Avery smiled. "You can do your play-by-play."

"Not funny." I gripped the back of my neck. "They're going to see you."

"I'm doing a project, a twelve-days-of-Christmas project. That's my alibi."

Before I could say another word, she rolled into the back and hockey-stopped by the sinks. Then she popped a wheelie and did a slow three-sixty.

I looked over at the fridge. Tarantula had her back to Avery. Down the line, Ratio was working the register and . . .

Suddenly, Tiki raced past me and headed for Avery.

"Tiki, what are you doing? Stop!"

She didn't.

"Tiki, get out of there!"

Too late.

"What are you doing, young lady?" Donatella snapped.

"I thought Avery got caught," Tiki answered.

This can't be happening. This can't be happening. This can't be happening.

"Got caught doing what?" Bunion said, turning from the serving line. "What are you two doing back here?"

Tiki glanced my way. Donatella saw.

"What is going on here?" Bunion waved her serving spoon from Avery to Tiki.

"Um, we were . . . we were playing a game," Tiki

stammered. She snort-laughed. "Yeah, we were playing a spy game—"

"Sweetheart, you're making a fool of yourself," Bunion said, cutting her off. "You think I was born yesterday?"

"Shut up, Tiki," Avery growled.

"Honest," Tiki kept talking. "We were playing—"

"Sweetheart, stop," Bunion interrupted again. She spun to me. "You're the wise guy who walks all over our clean tables every morning. You don't think we know who you are?"

I didn't. I didn't think they knew I even existed.

"Yikezy-wikezy," Tiki whimpered. She pressed her hands to her cheeks. "We're sorry, we're sorry, we're sorry." Her whimpers became cries. "There's a camera on the back of her chair. We've been . . ."

"A camera?" Tarantula stormed over. "Stop talking! All of you. Principal Darling's office. Let's go. Right now!"

Caught

The last time I was in Principal Darling's office was back in the spring when Hunter, Zachary, and I made the TouchCast vid. Principal Darling sat with us on the floor in front of her desk and asked us questions about the unit on climate change we'd been working on in Ms. Wright's class. When we finished, she let us sit in her chair and spin around as fast as we could.

No one was taking her chair for spins today.

I looked over at Diego. His head was down, so the blue-and-white eyes of his SpongeBob hat were looking back at me. Tiki sat beside him. She was no longer crying, but her chin still quivered. She wiped her tearstained cheeks with her shoulder sleeves. Avery was parked next to her. She had her elbow resting on her armrest and her head against her knuckles. She stared out the window.

I checked Principal Darling. She sat at her desk hunched over her laptop, emailing our parents. We needed to be picked up. We were being sent home.

"I thought you were getting in trouble," Tiki whispered to Avery. "I couldn't stand the sight—"

"Whatever, dude." Avery's eyes stayed on the window.

"This is all my fault. When I saw . . ."

"It's okay," Avery muttered.

But it wasn't okay. That's what I wanted to say to Tiki. *None of this would've happened if you hadn't panicked.*

"Disappointing," Principal Darling said. She stood up, rolled her chair around her desk, and sat down next to Diego. "You involved Red?"

The words were aimed at me.

Red wasn't with us. After we got caught, Red refused to leave the booth. He sat swaying back and forth with his hands behind his neck and his arms squeezing his head. He kept saying, "Stop, stop, stop." Ms. Yvonne had to come get him and take him to her office.

"Red was only lookout," I said.

"Lookout?" Principal Darling said. "What does that mean?"

"All he did was sit at the booth," I said. "His job was to keep an eye out for teachers, but he really . . . Tiki was our real lookout."

"Did Red think he was the lookout?"

"Yes."

"Did he think he was involved?"

"Yes."

"Then he was involved." She shook her head. "So disappointing."

If you ever get caught doing something stupid, I hope you have the good sense to admit it.

Mom's words were on blast in my brain. I twisted a lock near my forehead at its root. I had to come clean. I had to admit . . .

"This was my idea," Tiki blurted. "I was the one who came up with the plan."

"We all agreed to it," Diego said. "It was everyone's idea."

"No," Tiki said. "I came up with it first. I was the one who wanted—"

Avery cut her off. "It was everyone's idea."

"Enough," Principal Darling said, holding up a hand. "Here's what's going to happen. Tomorrow morning, we're all going to meet here. All of you, all of your parents. Then we'll get to the bottom of—"

Principal Darling didn't finish the sentence. She stared at her phone and shook her head.

"This is ridiculous," she said after a moment. "They have me out of the building every day this week. How do they expect me to be a principal if I'm never here?"

We weren't supposed to answer the question.

"This is going to have to wait until Friday morning." She looked at each of us. "All of you and all of your parents will be here Friday morning. Until then, you're not permitted to set foot in that cafeteria. If you get grab-and-go, someone will bring you your breakfast. During lunch, you'll be elsewhere. On Friday morning, there are going to be significant consequences."

The Hot Seat, Again

Mom didn't say a word the whole ride home. She didn't look my way either. Not even a peek out of the corner of her eye.

When we turned onto Key Place, I thought she might stop the car in the middle of the street again, but she didn't.

Mom was in total principal mode. Just like she'd been in total principal mode since she'd picked me up. Her lips were pursed, and she was tapping the steering wheel with her fingertips. She was nodding, too.

I see Mom in principal mode all the time, but I've only seen her in principal mode because of *me* twice. Once was in second grade when I threw a basketball across the gym after we lost a close game. She made me call the other team's coach and apologize. Then she didn't let me play in the next three games. The other time was last spring when I posted comments she said I shouldn't have. She took away the Wi-Fi password for a month. I was only allowed to use the Internet when she was in the room.

This was the third time.

As soon as we pulled into the driveway, I unlocked my door.

Mom relocked it.

I was in the hot seat. Again.

"Every last detail," she said, pointing her keys at the house. "When we get inside, you sit down at the kitchen counter, and you start writing. I want every last detail."

"I told Principal Darling the truth," I said.

"You better have."

"I mean . . . I did what you said. Like when kids at your school get busted in the act."

"You better have," she repeated. "I can't believe you involved Red."

"Do you know what he said?"

"I'm not interested right now."

"Please, it's—"

"Rip, I said—"

"No." The word came out louder than I meant it to. "Please. It's something he said this morning. It's really good."

"Rip, I know you're working me right now, and I don't appreciate it."

"Before school," I said anyway, "when we were playing tinfoil basketball in the cafeteria, Red—"

"Tinfoil basketball? Why do I have a feeling I'm not going to like what that is?"

"Red used the expression 'pushing the envelope,'" I said. "He said we were pushing the envelope too far."

"Red said that?"

I nodded. "Mr. Acevedo taught us what it meant a few weeks ago. Red learned it. He's catching on to things so much faster."

"Not fast enough to know not to go along with this."

I lifted my legs so that my shins pressed against the glove box. "Mom, he didn't do anything."

"Yes, he did." She backhanded the side of my knee. "Put your legs down."

I picked my water bottle out of the cup holder and squirted what was left into my mouth.

"Operation Food Fight?" she said. "You come up with that?"

"We all did." I wiped my chin. "Tiki came up with the name."

"Honey, I told you point-blank it wasn't going to be pleasant for the parent of the next kid who got caught doing something like this. Point-blank."

"I know."

"Now I'm that parent." She pinched her thumb and index finger together. "I thought you would've had a teeny-tiny bit more sense than this."

I let out a puff. "I know."

"This is such an inconvenience, Rip. I have my School Leadership Team meeting on Friday mornings, and the SLT didn't meet last week because of the holiday. Now we're not going to meet again. Because of you." She tapped the console with her fist. "I expected so much better from you, Rip. So much better."

Something's Up

"Something's up," Red said when we got to Room 208 the next morning.

When Red says something's up, something usually is. Though this time, even I could see something was up.

Mr. Acevedo was wearing dress pants and a button-down shirt. A blue sport jacket hung across the armrest of his chair. It was the first time all year he wasn't wearing jeans.

As the other kids filed in, everyone had a reaction.

"Looking dope, Mr. Acevedo," Attie said.

When Melissa arrived, she checked the number on the door to make sure she had the right room, just like she did the first time she'd laid eyes on Mr. Acevedo.

"Who died?" Declan said as he walked in. "What time's the funeral?"

This was bad. Seriously, seriously bad.

"So no one freaks out," Mr. Acevedo said, after most of the kids were in the room, "let's start off with CC today."

A few moments later, we were seated in the meeting area.

"What's the story?" Miles asked.

"Spill it, Teach," Declan said. "What's up?"

Mr. Acevedo smiled. "What makes you think something's up?"

Declan, who was lying in the bathtub, popped to his feet and stood in the tub. "Let me count the ways," he said. "One, you're not smiling. Well, you are right now, but you weren't until a second ago. Two, you're sitting in your chair. You never sit in your chair at CC. You always sit on the carpet. Three, you have your thermos. You never bring your thermos to CC. Four—"

"You can stop now." Mr. Acevedo held up his hand. "You're right, something's up."

I looked around. Avery was parked by the door. She was twisting a paper clip in her lap. Her head was down. Diego sat on the floor beside her. His head was down, too, and all I could see was his blue-and-yellow one-eyed Minion hat. Tiki was a couple beanbags to my left. Her arms were crossed, and her fists were clenched. She was staring at Mr. Acevedo. Red sat in a chair on the far side of the couch. He was spinning a pen cap on the cover of the composition notebook in his lap. Ms. Yvonne was beside him with her hand on his back.

"I have to attend a couple meetings today," Mr. Acevedo

said, pulling back his hair. "I'm not a big fan of meetings during our class time, but these are meetings I need to attend."

My brain was bursting. The meetings were about us. The meetings had to be about us. We got him in trouble. Big trouble. We *pushed the envelope* too far.

"RJE is experiencing growing pains," he said. "That's no secret. So I've been *asked* to meet with some people today. Without going into too many details, we're trying to get to the root of a few of these growing pains and maybe find a few solutions." He bongo-drummed his legs. "But don't you worry, I'll be back in my jeans tomorrow."

One on One

Twenty-three hours and forty-two minutes later . . .

Mr. Acevedo was in Room 208 wearing the jeans he'd worn to school every day except for yesterday.

"Who's my first victim?" he asked.

I was his first victim. He'd told me that when Red and I had walked in this morning. I was having the first Where I Read conference.

We met on the rug. I sat on a beanbag. He sat on the floor.

"Let's get right down to this," he said, strumming the carpet. "Let's see what you got."

I pulled the stapled papers from my folder. "I didn't always keep them as I went along," I said, handing them over.

"You weren't the only one."

"I don't like keeping reading logs, Mr. Acevedo."

"I'm not a big fan of them either," he said without looking up, "but these weren't reading logs in the traditional sense."

"I hate when . . . I mean . . . I'm sorry."

"It's all good, Rip."

You're not allowed to say *hate* at RJE.

"I don't *like* when I have to write about what I'm reading," I said.

"Neither do I." He glanced up. "Where's 'the Hood'?"

I smiled. "The hood of Mom's car in the Home Depot parking lot."

"Why'd you decide to read there?"

"I didn't want to look at Christmas decorations. We were parked right near the entrance, so Mom said I could stay by the car. She knew I'd be fine."

"Reading while you wait—a great reading strategy." He

tapped the page again. "*Can I See Your I.D.?* Cool book. Which story did you like the best?"

"The first one," I said, "the one about the kid who took the New York City subway train for a joyride."

After I finished *A Wrinkle in Time*, I picked up *Can I See Your I.D.?* Gavin had posted a review on Yo! Read This! so I decided to give it a shot. I was glad I did.

"I like that you're reading different genres," Mr. Acevedo said. "Keep it up."

"Thanks." I brushed the locks from my forehead and let out a puff. "Did we get you in trouble?"

"What makes you ask that?"

"You were dressed up yesterday. You had to go to those meetings."

"You thought that was because of you?"

"Well, yeah." I nodded. "We got you in trouble for Operation Food Fight, right?"

"Rip, those meetings had nothing to do with that." He tightened an earring. "I got me in trouble. I pulled a little switcheroo a few weeks ago."

"Switcheroo?"

"Yeah," he said with a half smile, "but it was absolutely worth it. I've already gotten pretty good at taking care of myself around here." He tapped my foot. "Tell me about Rip Hamilton."

"Rip Hamilton?" I made a face.

"That's where your nickname comes from, right?"

"Yeah, Rip Hamilton."

"Tell me about him. I know he played college ball at UConn and won an NBA title with the Pistons. Tell me some things I don't know."

I smiled a Red-like basketball smile. "In high school, he played on a traveling all-star team with Kobe Bryant," I said. "They were roommates sometimes."

"Nice."

"When UConn beat Duke to win the NCAA Tournament, he was the Most Outstanding Player of the Final Four. Then he was drafted by the Washington Wizards."

"Do you know who he played with on the Wizards?"

"Michael Jordan!"

"That's right." He looked back at my sheets. "*The Walking Dead*, huh?"

"Is it okay that I'm reading another graphic novel?"

Mr. Acevedo chuckled. "A little different from *A Wrinkle in Time*, right?"

"A little." I shook out my hair. "Xander's brother gave me the whole series."

"Your mom's okay with you reading them?"

"As long as I don't get nightmares or want to sleep in her bed."

Mr. Acevedo laughed. "Sounds reasonable." He tapped my foot again. "So we're good, Rip?"

"We're good."

"That makes me happy. Big game at Walker tomorrow."

"I'm bringing it."

"That makes me even happier."

Bench Mob!

From the opening tip, our starters looked out of sync against the Walker Wolves. On our first possession, Keith threw a pass out of bounds. A couple plays later, Jason missed a wide-open layup. The next time we had the ball, Mehdi traveled. Then he traveled again.

Luckily, the Wolves didn't take advantage of our sloppy start. They were ready for our press—word had gotten around—but they couldn't put the ball in the basket either. Four minutes in, the game was still scoreless.

I looked down the bench. Coach Acevedo needed to bring in the second unit. It was only a matter of time before the Wolves went on a run. We didn't want to fall behind on the road. He needed to shake things up, but I was done trying to figure out Coach Acevedo's—

"Let's go, Bench Mob!" he said.

"Yes!" I leaped off the bench and hammer-fisted the air.

"We need a different look out there," Coach Acevedo said. "Let's shake things up."

Shake things up. It was like he read my mind.

As I took the court, Tiki headed my way with her fist held out. I gave her a pound, a real pound. When our knuckles met, so did our eyes.

"Zwibble," she said, smiling. She then blew a bubble and scooted to the bench.

I waved Wil, Maya, Chris, and Jeffrey together. We football-huddled near the foul line.

"The Bench Mob takes control," I said. "Just like we did against Fairlawn. We're all involved on offense, we're all involved on defense. Let's do this."

I took the inbounds and brought the ball upcourt. When I crossed the timeline, I hit Wil on the left and cut right, setting a screen for Maya. She ran off my shoulder and caught Wil's pass by the top of the key. I kept on moving toward the corner and set a back screen for Chris as Maya threw a pass to Jeffrey inside the paint.

"Roll, roll," I said to Chris.

He ran off my pick, and just like I'd hoped, Jeffrey spotted him along the baseline and fed him the ball. Chris sank the layup.

"That's how we roll!" I leaped.

All five Clifton United had touched the ball.

"Bench Mob!" Red, Max, and Tiki chanted on the sidelines. They stood on the first row of the bleachers and waved towels. "Bench Mob!"

"Find your man!" I said to my teammates. "Press, press!"

With my basketball eyes, I spotted my man breaking downcourt for a long pass. I could tell he thought he had me beat, but he didn't know he was up against the Gnat. At midcourt, he stopped for the pass, but he didn't jump for it. I leaped in front of him and snatched the ball out of the air.

Suddenly, in my head, I was back in my bedroom, making magical moves with my Nerf. As soon as I landed, I put the ball on the floor. With my head up, I charged downcourt, weaving around one man and darting past another. At the foul line, I crossover-dribbled and then drove down the lane. But I left my feet a step too soon, so instead of putting up a layup, I had to shoot a teardrop. As the ball left my fingers, a Wolves big man smacked my arm and knocked my body.

Tweet! Tweet!

"Good if it goes!" the ref called, raising his arm.

It went.

"Who's your daddy?" I shouted.

"Bench Mob!" our entire bench cheered. "Bench Mob!"

"Way to go, Mason Irving!" Red jumped in circles.

I raced to the sideline and met him with a double high five as he hopped off the bleachers.

"Roll left, roll right," we chanted. "Slap right, slap left." We jumped, bumped hips, and on the landing . . .

"Boo-yah!"

* * *

At halftime, we didn't meet as a team, but it wasn't because we were up 18–8 and didn't need to. Well, maybe it was a little, but it was really because Coach Acevedo said he had to meet with someone. So Mehdi's dad stayed with us in the gym as we shot around.

Right before the start of the second half, we found out who Coach Acevedo had to meet with: Avery. When he came back into the gym, she was with him.

"Avery Goodman!" Red shouted. He spun to me. "Avery Goodman's here, Mason Irving."

Avery wheeled onto the court and hockey-stopped by Red. "I'm friggin' pumped," she said, smacking her armrest. "My first away game."

"Way to go," I said.

She looked my way. "Dude, I heard you're putting on a show."

"You'll have to see for yourself," I said.

"Check these out," she said, grabbing her bag off the back of her chair. "I designed them myself."

She reached in and pulled out a navy T-shirt. Across the front in yellow letters, it read BENCH MOB.

"Boss!" I said.

"There's one for everyone." She tossed the shirt to Red.

He caught it and hopped from foot to foot. "Boss, Avery Goodman."

* * *

Wearing our new Bench Mob T-shirts, Wil, Maya, Chris, Jeffrey, Red, Max, and I stood on the front row of the bleachers as Clifton United's first unit took the floor to start the second half.

We scored on our first possession, extending our lead.

"U-ni-ted!" we cheered. "U-ni-ted!"

But just like in the first half, the Wolves were able to break our press, keep our first unit off balance, and take advantage of our turnovers. Five minutes into the second half, they'd trimmed our lead to six.

So Coach Acevedo went back to the Bench Mob.

I pulled off my shirt and threw it at Avery. "Hold this," I said.

"Dude," she said, batting it away.

Then Jeffrey threw his shirt at her. Then Chris did. Then Maya did.

"That's the thanks I get?" she said, ducking and smiling.

I scooped up the basketball by the scorer's table and headed onto the court.

"Hold on a sec," Coach Acevedo said. He finger-waved the Bench Mob back. "I'm shaking things up again. Wil, we're going to have you stay on the bench a little longer." He pointed to Tiki. "You stay in and play the two guard." He spun to me. "Rip, you're our floor leader. Run the point."

"You got it, Coach." I pounded the basketball.

The new-look Bench Mob took the floor. Tiki and I were playing together.

"Go, Takara Eid!" Red shouted. "Go, Mason Irving!"

I took the inbounds pass from under our basket and dribbled up the floor. Crossing midcourt, I spotted Maya, running along the baseline. From beyond the three-point circle, I whipped an off-the-dribble, laser-like pass that buzzed by five outstretched hands. Maya caught my bullet, and without stopping, she flipped up the ball and sank a reverse layup.

"Boo-yah!" I hammer-fisted the air.

"Great pass!" Maya yelled.

The Wolves inbounded quickly—that's how they had been breaking the press against our first unit.

But not against the Bench Mob.

Tiki was on that pass the moment it left the Wolves player's fingers. Out of nowhere, she plucked the ball from the air. But her momentum carried her to the corner. As she was about to fall out of bounds, she spun and underhand-passed to me. I caught the ball, and once again, I saw that Maya was about to be wide open. But before I threw the rock her way, my basketball eyes spotted Tiki, bolting for the basket. I fired a one-handed bounce pass. She caught it chest high and buried the layup.

"Bam!" Red jumped in circles. "Oh, yeah, Mason Irving!"

"Dude!" Avery popped a wheelie and did a three-sixty.

No lie, we were looking like a middle school team. No, we were looking *better* than a middle school team.

"Prestanderous!" Tiki shouted. She raced up to me and held out both fists.

I gave her a double pound.

"BTW," Tiki said, "*prestanderous* isn't my word. It's a word a kid made up on this show I love."

* * *

We won by seventeen. Thanks to the Bench Mob.

Clifton United was now 5–0.

Sentencing

Friday morning. Principal Darling's office.

"Let's get right down to this," she said once everyone was seated around the conference table. "I don't think any one of us wants to be here longer than we have to be."

Mom and I sat at the far end of the table. Mom was doodling on her yellow legal pad, I was staring at Red. He sat facing the door with his shoulders hunched, and by the way his arms moved, I could tell he was pinky-thumb-tapping his bouncing legs. Ms. Yvonne was on one side of Red, Suzanne on the other. Suzanne had her hand on his shoulder.

"Sit still," Diego's mom said to Diego, who was swinging his hat strings.

Diego put his head down and rested his chin on the table.

"We'll start with you, Rip," Principal Darling said.

I let out a long puff. I would've bet my throwback Iverson jersey I was going to have to speak first.

If you ever get busted doing something stupid, I hope you have the good sense to admit it.

Mom's words were again on full blast inside my head.

"We broke the rules," I said. "We understood what would happen if we got caught. We all did."

I didn't make eye contact with anyone as I spoke. Except for Mr. Acevedo, who was next to Principal Darling.

"We decided not to use a cell phone because of what happened last year," I went on. "But we all knew it was the same thing. We all did. We—"

"It was the first time I ever felt included," Tiki interrupted.

"Tiki, you'll have your chance," Principal Darling said. "Please be patient."

"I'd never been included before." She kept going anyway. "Not like this. It was the first time I ever felt like I was part of something."

"Tiki, please," Principal Darling said. "I need you to wait—"

"It's okay," I said, nodding. "I was almost done."

I wasn't. Not even close. But for the first time, I wanted to hear what Tiki had to say.

"I'd never been to a school where the kids knew the lunch ladies' names, and I've been to a lot of schools. A lot." She was . . . whimpering? "They just wanted the Lunch Bunch back. I wanted to help them. They cared about them so much. How could I not help?"

I checked Tiki's parents. Both her mom and her dad were here. Her dad was wearing a polo shirt, but in my mind's eye, I'd always pictured him wearing a suit and having a beard. But he didn't have a beard either. He had his hand on top of Tiki's, which was resting on the table. Whenever her voice cracked, he squeezed her fingers.

"The funny thing is," Tiki said, "Rip doesn't even like me." She looked my way. "You don't. You hated me from the moment I walked into . . ." She covered her mouth. "Sorry for using the *H* word."

"No, I didn't," I whispered. I folded my arms and shook my head. "I didn't."

"You let me be a lookout with Red," she said. "I knew we really weren't doing much, but I didn't care. You were letting me be a part of it."

I peeked over at Red. His face was squinched into a knot. Suzanne was rubbing his neck. I lowered my hands, locked my fingers under the table, and pressed them against my leg.

"Then I ruined it." Tiki started crying. "For everyone. I blew it."

Tiki's dad began to cry, too. Tears streamed down both cheeks. He didn't make any effort to wipe them away.

"We want the Lunch Bunch back, Principal Darling," I said. "RJE isn't the same without them. Lunch isn't . . . It doesn't feel like RJE anymore."

Red opened his eyes. "Everyone misses Ms. Eunice, Ms. Carmen, Ms. Joan, Ms. Audrey, and Ms. Liz," Red said. "Takara Eid misses the Lunch Bunch, and she never met the Lunch Bunch."

The grown-ups chuckled.

"The cafeteria used to be awesome." I unlocked my fingers. "The Lunch Bunch used to play music during grab-and-go, and they sang and danced when they served lunch. The food was a gazillion times better, too."

"The food now is foul," Avery said.

"Sometimes they got dressed up in costumes," I went on,

"and sometimes Ms. Audrey and Ms. Eunice would play kickball and four square with us at recess."

"They taught us things," Diego said.

"They did." I nodded. "We learned all about landfill garbage, recycling, and composting. We compost at home now. Right, Mom?"

"We do," she said. "Rip's turned into quite the stickler. I don't dare put something in the garbage that can be recycled or composted."

"Thanks, Rip," Principal Darling said. She turned to Avery. "Is there anything you want to add?"

Avery motioned to me with a twisted paper clip. "Rip said everything."

"You have nothing at all to say?" her mother asked.

"What do you want me to say?" Avery shrugged. "The Lunch Bunch was like family."

"Diego, what about you?" Principal Darling asked.

He shook his head. He held the bottoms of his hat strings so they wouldn't swing.

"Red?"

"No, Principal Darling." Red squinched his face again. "No, no, no."

"Do any of the parents want to add anything?" She looked around the table, but no one spoke up. "Just so you kids know," Principal Darling said, "all the grown-ups here have spoken with me already. We're all on the same page." She faced my mom. "Lesley, I'm not the only principal here. Anything I may have missed?"

"You five are very lucky," Mom said, morphing into principal mode. "Very lucky. This is not how this plays out in most schools." She tapped her pad with the eraser end of her pencil. "You are very lucky you go to a school like RJE. You are very lucky to have parents who care like we do. Just imagine for a moment being a kid at this meeting without a parent sitting next to you." She put down the pencil. "Respect how lucky you are. Respect your good fortune."

"Thanks." Principal Darling pulled a paper from her folder. "Everyone here appreciates your willingness to accept responsibility for your actions. It makes all this slightly less unpleasant, though only slightly. We all agree a harsh punishment in this situation isn't going to do much good, but I am accountable to the district office, the school board, and the community." She clasped her hands and rocked forward. "So here's what's going to happen: immediately following this meeting, the five of you will go home."

Tiki covered her mouth. "I'm sorry." She turned to her mother. "I'm sorry."

"You'll all come back to school on Monday. Rip, Red, and Tiki, the three of you don't play ball this weekend."

"This was the only game you could make." Tiki turned to her father. "Now you'll never get to see me play."

Principal Darling shook her head."You can't miss school

on Friday and then play ball on Saturday," she said. "That's not how it works."

"I'm sorry, Pop," Tiki said.

Tears ran down his cheeks again. He shut his eyes and nodded.

"I'm sorry, Pop," she repeated.

"It's okay, Takara Eid," Red said.

He stood up. He pressed his elbows to his sides and hunched his shoulders. Then he walked around the table to Tiki. He leaned over and hugged her.

"It's okay, Takara Eid," Red said again.

Then he shuffled back to his seat, sat down, and pinky-thumb-tapped his leg.

Suzanne squeezed his neck and smiled. I'd never seen her smile like that before.

"Rip and Red," Principal Darling said, "the two of you aren't allowed in the building early anymore." She looked from Red to me. "Your morning pass is revoked until after Christmas. When we get back from vacation, the five of us and Mr. Acevedo are all going to meet and figure out what to do next." She turned to Mr. Acevedo. "I believe you're up now. Take it away."

Mr. Acevedo strummed the table. "After the break," he said, "we're going to start planning for our community garden. When I interviewed for this position last summer, I was asked if I'd be interested in spearheading the community garden initiative, and I said absolutely. Now we have the students who are going to help make it happen."

"I like this punishment already," Diego said, smiling. He swung his strings and dodged his mother's fingers.

"It's not a punishment, Diego." Mr. Acevedo brushed some hair off his face. "That's not how I see this. I see this as a privilege with a bit of retribution, and if you don't know what *retribution* means, look it up when you get home."

I had no idea what *retribution* meant other than that it had to do with our punishment that wasn't a punishment.

"Thank you, Mr. Acevedo," Principal Darling said. She looked around the table. "In the springtime, I'll reach out to the Lunch Bunch. Perhaps they can visit on School Lunch Hero Day."

"Sweet," Diego said. "Thanks, Principal Darling."

"We're not the only school in the county having issues with this new food service company," she said. "We've reached out to their management. We're trying to see what we can do about it. We need them to be part of our community. If they're unwilling or unable to, then next year we'll need to go in a different direction. A tried-and-true one."

A Girl in My Bedroom!

I tossed my purple teddy toward the foot of the bed and turned onto my side. I grabbed my pillow and—

Tiki stood in the middle of my room.

"Whoa!" I shot up. "What are you doing here?" I pulled the comforter up to my neck.

"Your mom let me in," she said.

"I was sleeping!" I checked the clock. "It's eight-forty-five in the morning."

I blinked hard. I wasn't dreaming. Tiki was really standing in front of my workstation staring right at me. How long had she been here? I reached under the comforter and made sure my glow-in-the-dark smiley-face boxers still covered my butt. Then I grabbed all the stuffed animals I could reach and pushed them into the space between the mattress and the wall.

"I'm sorry for getting us caught," she said.

"I know. You said that."

76ers

"I couldn't stand seeing my friends getting in trouble."

"What are you doing here, Tiki?" I gripped the end of my comforter. "It's Sunday morning. Don't you think it's a little weird—"

"I'm so bummidy-bummed-bummed-bummed we lost yesterday. We should've destroyed Yaeger. So much for going undefeated."

"Did you call before you came over?" I asked.

"Cypress Village won again. They're only a game behind us." She shook her hands at me and then pretended to run in place. "That play where I stole the ball in the corner and threw it to you, and you passed it back to me—that was like the greatest pass ever-ever-ever-after."

"Thanks." I blinked hard again.

"I real-zee-fa-real-zee wanted to play ball with you again." She stepped toward my bed. "It makes me so sad—" She stopped midsentence and picked up the purple teddy. "He's cute."

"Can you put him down?"

"What's his name?"

I stared at her thumb with the bitten-off nail and the scabbed-over cuticle. It was touching my bear's mouth. "He doesn't have a name."

"He's your fave-a-fave." She held him to her chest. "How can he not have a name?"

"I don't have a favorite—"

"He would be my fave, too." She flexed her eyebrows. "I used to have tons of stuffed animals. Now all I have is Monroe, my giraffe."

She put the purple teddy on the bed. I snatched him away and put him by my pillow.

"I like it so much better like this," she said.

"Like what?"

"When you don't hate me." She sat down on my bed.

"What are you doing?" I brought my knees to my chest and inched toward the wall.

"It's so stressful not getting along with people."

"You're on my bed, Tiki."

"When I don't get along—"

"This is so weird."

"Everything's weird." She stood back up and headed for my trophy shelf.

"What are you doing now?"

"What's this one for?" She pointed to the bronze trophy of a player kicking a ball.

"Second-grade soccer. Everyone got one."

"This one?" She picked up the tall, gold-colored basketball one.

"Third-grade select." I wrapped my arms around my knees and pulled them closer. "Can you put it down?"

"Is this one your fave-a-fave?" She tapped the front plate. "It says GNAT."

"That's my nickname."

She put the trophy back. "Did your mom take away your password?"

"What?"

"Red says that when you get in trouble, your mom takes away your Wi-Fi password."

I let out a puff. "No."

"Zwibble."

"Can you stop saying that already?"

"That's my password." She blew the hair off her forehead and hand-brushed it to the side. "Do you know why that's my favorite word?"

I didn't answer. She was going to tell me anyway.

"When I was little, I used to think I was going to get kidnapped. I thought aliens disguised as my mom were going to take me away. So whenever my mom picked me up at school—especially at a new school—I was always terrified. I didn't think it was really her. So we came up with a word. Our own password. That's how I knew it was her. Now *Zwibble*'s my password for everything, except on sites where they make you have a number or character or—"

"Tiki, I need to go to the bathroom."

"Zwibble, zwibble, zwibble." She snort-laughed.

"I need to go to the bathroom," I said again.

"Okay."

I motioned to the door.

"OMG-eepers-creepers." She smacked her cheeks. "You're not wearing any clothes! I can't believe—"

"Yes, I am!"

"Embarrassment city! I can't believe—"

"I'm wearing clothes!"

"Phew!" She pretended to wipe sweat from her brow. "Could you imagine if you didn't have any clothes on this whole time?"

She headed for the door, but before she walked out, she stopped and turned around. Then for what felt like the longest time—but was probably only a few seconds—she just stared.

"You are so weird, Tiki." I motioned for her to go again.

"Good-bye, Mason Irving."

Gone

Red and I stood outside the entrance to RJE with the rest of the kids and waited for the building to open.

Well, I was standing. Red was spinning around one of the poles for the new fence being installed and bumping my shoulder each time he passed. It was a little annoying—and got more annoying after he knocked my granola bar into a puddle—but I wasn't about to say anything. Red was banging into me and not freaking out. That never used to happen.

"What's the deal?" Zachary said, walking over with the twins. "No more early pass?"

"No more early pass," I said.

"Do you know where Tiki is?" Ana asked.

I leaned away from Red's next shoulder bump. "I have no idea."

"This is the first day she didn't attack us," Lana said.

"What does that mean?"

"Every morning, as soon as she sees us, she runs over. But she's not very good at stopping."

Zachary flicked his hand near my face. "You wouldn't know that since you had your pass."

"It's kind of refreshing having a day off from her," Lana said, "if you know what I mean."

"I know what you mean," I said. "I know exactly what you mean."

* * *

"So we have some news this morning," Mr. Acevedo said at the start of CC.

He sat in his spot on the rug and looked around the

meeting area. He made eye contact with a few of the kids, including me.

"I was hoping to find some words of wisdom to go along with the news," he said, "but I couldn't find the right ones, so I'm just going to say it."

I checked Red. He was on a beanbag, tapping his leg. Ms. Yvonne sat on the floor beside him.

"Spill it, Teach," Declan said. "What's going on?"

Mr. Acevedo pulled back his hair and exhaled a deep breath. "Tiki's no longer in Room 208."

I rocked.

"She's not going to be at RJE anymore," he added.

"Tiki's gone?" Diego grabbed his hat strings.

"Did something happen to her?" Lana asked.

"Is she okay?" Piper said.

"Hold on, hold on, hold on." Mr. Acevedo held out both hands. "Before you get any ideas, it's nothing like that."

Too late. My brain was bursting with ideas.

How were we going to beat Cypress Village and Millwood? We needed her. Clifton United was . . .

I hit Pause inside my head.

Was that why she came over? Was that why she was acting even weirder than usual?

"Tiki was never going to be here for long," Mr. Acevedo said.

"Why didn't she say anything?" Ana asked.

"Because she said kids treated her differently when they knew she was leaving," Mr. Acevedo said. "She and I talked about it. As a matter of fact, she said *everyone* treated her differently when they knew she was leaving."

I grabbed the locks above my neck and squeezed. She really did move around a lot. RJE was just another stop.

"Tiki's family had to move out of state," Mr. Acevedo said. "Mr. Eid is starting a new job right after the first of the year."

"Pop," Red said. "Takara Eid called her father Pop."

"Thanks, Red." Mr. Acevedo nodded once. "She did. They're moving this week so they can settle in before he starts."

"Takara Eid's pop told us they were moving," Red said.

Everyone faced him.

"He did," Red said. "At the meeting in Principal Darling's office, Takara Eid's pop told us they were moving."

"Dude, no, he didn't," Avery said.

"When did he say that?" Diego asked.

"Takara Eid said that whenever her family is about to move, her pop always shaves. Takara Eid's pop didn't have his beard. Takara Eid's pop shaved."

Whenever my family is about to move again, Pop shaves.

I rocked again.

I stared at Red. He knew at the meeting on Friday. He realized it then.

Our eyes met.

"Takara Eid told us she was moving, Mason Irving."

Table for Four

"Peas?" I scooped some off my tray with my spork. "You call these peas?"

"They look like soggy booger balls," Diego said.

"They look nasty!" Red said.

We were back in our booth. Diego and Red were across from me. Avery was parked at the end. I had the side to myself. Our usual spots, usual before Tiki.

"Why do they even bother serving them?" Diego said. "They're only going to end up on the floor." He put some peas on his spork and flicked them at me. They flew past my shoulder. "See what I'm saying?"

"Do you think we were part of why she moved?" I asked.

"Mr. Acevedo said it was because of her father's job," Diego said.

"I know what he said, but . . . I don't know."

I looked over at the service area. It was the first day we were allowed back in the cafeteria. I thought it was going to be weird with the lunch ladies, but it wasn't. None of them said anything or even gave us a look. Ratio might have half smiled when she swiped my card, but I could've imagined that.

I stabbed my spork into a not-so-crispy chicken tender and took a bite. Before I finished chewing, the rest of it was back on my tray.

"I should've gotten the meatball sub," I said.

"No, you shouldn't have." Diego opened his sandwich. "These aren't meatballs. These are meat marbles."

"No, that's bread and sauce," Avery said.

"She's been to eight schools," I said.

"About to be nine," Diego added.

"I would friggin' hate moving around like that," Avery said.

"I would friggin' hate moving around like that, too," Red said.

We all laughed.

"What's so funny?" he asked.

"Dude, you said *friggin'* and *hate* in the same sentence," Avery said. "That was probably the first time you said either word."

"Yo, that was messed up seeing her dad cry like that," Diego said. "It made me want to cry."

"You and me both," Avery said.

"I never believed her," I said softly. "That she moved around like that."

"Some best friend you were," Diego said.

"I wasn't her best friend. Red was."

"No, I wasn't, Mason Irving. Takara Eid said you were her best friend."

I looked at Avery.

"Dude, you were," she said.

"And you didn't even like her." Diego dipped his spork back into his peas and flipped some more at me.

This time they landed in my lap.

I reached for his sub.

"Don't start!" Avery slammed her hand on the table. "I'm not playing."

I laughed. Then I snort-laughed. Like Tiki.

Avery held up her arms, flexed her eyebrows, and snort-laughed, too.

Then Red snort-laughed.

"Wait," Diego said. He slid out of the booth and reached for his milk carton. He took a sip and then snort-laughed the milk out his nose and mouth. "Zwibble!"

Alone

You are so weird, Tiki.

The words are on repeat inside my head.

I was supposed to be reading. *Safety Behind Bars* was open on my desk, but I'd been staring at the same page since Choice began.

I put a stickie on top of Hershel and Rick's conversation and picked up my pen.

You are so weird, Tiki.

You are so weird, Tiki.

You are so weird, Tiki.

You are so weird, Tiki.

Why did that have to be the last thing I ever said to her? Why did . . .

Mr. Acevedo knocked on my desk.

I flinched.

"Let's have a conversation in the hall," he said.

He tucked the picture book he was holding under his

arm and grabbed a couple beanbag chairs. A moment later, we were sitting on them side by side against the wall outside Room 208.

"Here." He handed me the picture book. "Take a little break from *The Walking Dead* and read this."

I checked the cover. "Another Jacqueline Woodson book?"

Earlier in the year, Mr. Acevedo had given me one of her books, a novel. It was about this kid named Mel, who was a lot like me.

"It's very different," he said. "It's about a new girl in class and how . . . Well, you'll see."

"Thanks." I leaned the book against my chest and let

out a puff. "Yesterday, when you told us Tiki moved, the first thing . . ." I twisted a lock near my forehead. "I thought about our last two games. That was the first thing that came into my head. Pretty crappy, right? The first thing I thought about was how were we going to win without her."

Mr. Acevedo nodded once. "So what do you want to do with that?"

I faced him.

"What do you want to do with that?" he said again. "Do you just want to let that eat at you? Or do you want to do something about it? What *can* you do about it?"

Leading the Way

With two games to go in the season, we faced Cypress Village at home. They were red-hot. After dropping their first two games, they'd won their next four and were now only a game behind us in the standings. Since only the top two teams made the playoffs, this *was* a playoff game.

"Let's go, Red!" I hard-clapped as he headed to the foul line for his pregame tradition. "Let's go, Twenty-Four!"

I looked over at the stage. Mehdi's dad was standing by the steps handing out blue-and-gold UNITED signs. Suzanne and Mom were opening folding chairs for the other parents. Noah, Melissa, Grace, Danny, Xander, Diego, and Avery sat on the front of the stage.

It was pretty awesome seeing Avery out of her chair.

"Show 'em how it's done, Blake Daniels!" she shouted with her hands cupped around her mouth.

Wearing his basketball smile, Red went through his free-throw ritual and took his underhanded foul shot.

Swish!

"Six for six!" I skipped out to meet him.

We went right into our handshake.

"Roll left, roll right. Slap right, slap left." We jumped, bumped hips, and on the landing . . .

"Boo-yah!" Clifton United cheered.

The team circled up in front of our bench.

"Two games to go." Coach Acevedo held up fingers. "We finish this season strong."

"We finish the season like we started the season." Keith pumped both fists. "Strong!"

"Clifton United goes thirteen deep." I clapped hard again. "That means we—"

"Twelve deep," Wil said. "Tiki's—"

"No." I cut him off. "Clifton United *still* goes thirteen deep." I pulled off my Bench Mob tee and pointed to my jersey.

I wasn't wearing my number thirty-two. I was wearing number three.

"That's Takara Eid's uniform." Red hopped from foot to foot. "Takara Eid wears number three."

I turned around. It still said EID across the back.

"Cool-a-rino!" Maya laughed.

"Perfectamundo!" Mehdi said.

"Super-dupers!" Jeffrey said.

"Prestanderous!" I said.

Coach Acevedo brushed some hair off his face. "Our Rookie of the Year is with us the whole season. Everyone contributes." He faced me. "You're our floor leader out there today, Rip. Let's get out there and take care of business."

* * *

"Back tap to me," I said to Dylan as he stepped into the circle. I spoke with my hand around my mouth. "I'm on the left."

I slide-stepped to Keith. "It's coming to me," I said. "As soon as he jumps, break for the hoop. Just go."

I found my spot on the circle. "I talk a lot," I said to the Cypress Village player with the fade and the titanium necklace. "Just so you know."

"Players, hold your spots." The referee raised the ball.

Tweet!

"Dylan Silver with the back tap to his point guard," I said as the ball went up, "and we're under way."

I put the rock by my hip, and with my basketball eyes I tracked Keith. Then I lobbed the ball over four red-and-white jerseys.

"Rip's going long," I announced. "Oh, what a look! Keith's got it. The layup . . . yes! Now, that's how you start a ballgame!"

I found my man and raced to him in the backcourt.

"Hands up!" I directed my teammates. "Who's got number five?"

Jason did, but he was a step slow getting to him. So that's where the inbounds went. But Dylan was able to get a fingertip on it, and I was all over the deflected pass. I grabbed it by the foul line extended, and dribbled back out.

"Go to the hole!" Coach Acevedo shouted from the sidelines. "Go to the hole."

He didn't need to say it twice (even though he did), and let me tell you, the move I made was like one I'd pulled off with my Nerf in my bedroom. If that coast-to-coast teardrop hoop I sank against Walker was the basket of my season, this was the basket of my life.

I went right at my man by the top of the key. I planted my left foot between his legs, lifted my toes, heel-pivoted, and rotated around him. A picture-perfect spin move! In the paint, I Euro-stepped (if you don't know what that means, look it up) by another player and went hard for the hoop. As I put up the layup, I got hit on the hand.

Tweet!

"And one!" The referee signaled as the ball fell through the net.

"The hoop and the harm!" I announced. "Oh, what a play by the Gnat. Where did that one come from?"

I charged over to our bench, and one by one I elbow-bashed Max, Maya, Wil, Chris, Jeffrey, Emily, and Red. I elbow-bashed Red the hardest.

"Where did that come from, Mason Irving?" He basketball-smiled.

I pinched out the Clifton United words on my jersey. "Who's your daddy?"

I then bolted for the stage and smacked hands with Noah, Melissa, Grace, Danny, Xander, Diego, and Avery.

"Let's go, number three," the referee said, holding out the ball. "Today."

I skip-ran back to the free-throw line and sank my foul shot.

"Whoosh!" the Bench Mob cheered.

"Hands up!" I directed my teammates again. "Press, press!"

We pressed. Cypress Village couldn't get the ball inbounds.

Tweet!

"Five-second violation," the ref called. "Blue ball on the side."

I hammer-fisted the air.

Clifton United was taking care of business.

Showdown!

The last time we'd played at Millwood it was a total disaster. We got our butts kicked, Red freaked out, and their Coach Crazy gave me nightmares for days. We definitely paid them back when we played them at RJE at the end of last season, but in my mind, that was only payback part one. I was out for even more today, and I was going to make sure Clifton United rose to the challenge.

Like last time, the bleachers on both sides of their high school–sized gym were packed with screaming fans waving orange-and-black towels, and techno music blasted from the speakers.

I slid over to the baseline to retie my kicks and checked Red. He was on the court warming up with the rest of the team. Then I looked over at Coach Crazy, who was already losing it.

"Not this time!" he shouted, smacking his clipboard and stalking the sidelines while the Millwood players shot around. "No way, no how! Not in our house!"

I clenched my fist and pounded the floor. No way, no how were we losing this game.

* * *

"You ready?" I asked.

"Ready as I'll ever be," Red said.

He stepped onto the court for his pregame free throw, and as soon as he did, the boos came loud and fast. Of course they did. The last time Red had stepped to the line against Millwood, he'd ended their season. But the boos didn't even faze him. Dribbling across the floor, Red kept on smiling his basketball smile.

You got this, Red. You got this.

But when he reached the top of the key, he stopped. Slowly, he turned in a circle. As he did, his smile grew even wider, and the boos grew louder. When he faced our bench, where the entire team was standing hand in hand, he waved.

I let go of Mehdi's hand and thumped my chest.

You got this, Red. Seven for seven. You got this.

Red stepped to the line and trapped the basketball soccer-style under his left foot. He pressed his earplugs deeper into his ears and took several breaths. Then he picked up the ball, squared his shoulders, and looked at the front rim. He dribbled three times—low, hard dribbles—and stood back up. He spun the ball until his fingers were on the right panel, looked at the rim again, extended his arms, and shot the ball.

Underhanded.

Swish!

* * *

"Let's circle up," I said to Mehdi, Jason, Dylan, and Keith. We put our arms around one another near center court. "We're playing our game today. We're calling the shots."

"This may be their court," Keith said, "but today it's our court."

I glanced over at the Millwood players lining up on the

circle. I recognized most of them from the last time we played. Mega-Man was jumping center again, Super-Size was pacing by the foul line, and their point guard was already swinging his elbows and looking my way.

Keep looking, Elbows.

"Clifton United goes thirteen deep." I patted the number three on my jersey. "Everyone contributes."

"Let's do this for Tiki," Jason said.

"Let's do it for the Rookie of the Year." Dylan thumped his chest.

I looked around the huddle and made eye contact with everyone. "Every little thing we do on this court matters." I put my hand in the middle. Everyone placed theirs on mine. "On three, team. One, two, three . . ."

"Team!"

On our first possession, Keith sank a jumper from the elbow, and we jumped out to a 2–0 lead. But we didn't jump ahead like we did in our other games. Millwood hung tough, just like we expected them to.

"Break that press!" the home fans chanted each time Millwood had the ball. "Break that press."

Our press was definitely working. We were getting stops,

but Millwood was finding holes and beating us down the floor. One time, Elbows whipped a pass to Super-Size, who sank a shot from inside the foul line. Another time, their guard with the glasses and the fingernails scratched my arm, dribbled around me, and drove past Jason and Mehdi for a basket.

"That's what I'm talking about!" Coach Crazy said. "That's how it's done."

But each time Millwood looked like they had our pressing defense figured out, someone on Clifton United stepped up. One time, Dylan picked off a pass and fed Jason for a bucket. Another time, Keith stripped Elbows clean and scored an easy deuce.

"What are you doing out there?" Coach Crazy banged his clipboard. "Play Millwood basketball! Stop embarrassing yourselves!"

"U-ni-ted!" Red and Max led the Bench Mob cheers. "U-ni-ted."

With eight minutes to go in the half and Clifton United leading 12–10, Coach Acevedo brought in the Bench Mob—Wil, Maya, Chris, Jeffrey, and Emily, who took my place with the second unit.

"You're playing against their scrubs," Coach Crazy barked. "Wipe the floor with them."

I traded fist bumps with Red when I reached the bench.

"You good?" I asked.

"Oh, yeah, Mason Irving."

I peeked down at Coach Crazy. "He's not getting to you?"

Red pressed his earplugs with his thumbs and shook his head.

On the court, the Bench Mob did its job. After Millwood scored, Maya hit a shot from inside the paint. Then, after Millwood scored again, Chris was fouled while taking a three-pointer. He made two of the free throws.

Then neither team scored for a while.

"You can't beat their benchwarmers?" Coach Crazy steamed. "You can't beat their scrubs?"

The next time Millwood had the ball, they broke our press with a long—lucky—baseball pass.

"Stomp them!" Coach Crazy swung his arms and kicked out a leg. "Stomp them!"

Suddenly, Elbows picked Chris's pocket, sneaking up from behind. He spun and found Mega-Man for a hoop.

"That's the way," Coach Crazy screamed. "Crush their spirit."

I checked Red. He was squinting, and his trembling fists were by his eyes.

"He's more nuts than ever," I said.

Red knuckle-pressed his earplugs.

After Millwood stopped us again, Jeffrey fouled Super-Size in the act of shooting.

"Make these," Coach Crazy ordered as Super-Size stepped to the line. "We're going for the kill. Make these!"

Super-Size did.

Millwood scored the last six points of the half and led 16–12 at the break.

* * *

At halftime, Coach Acevedo didn't have very much to say. He just told us to keep up the intensity and expect absolutely anything.

"They knocked you out of the game last season," I said to Keith, pumping him up as we retook the court.

He tugged my shoulder strap. "Time for us to knock them out of the playoffs," he said. "I want to see the Gnat."

"The Gnat is here."

We had to make stops. We had to break the momentum.

To start the second half, I went right at Fingernails as he brought the ball upcourt. I swiped at his dribble and got my hand on it, tapping the ball behind him. I scooted past him and beat Fingernails to the rock. I fired a pass to Keith, who scored a layup.

"Gnat!" He pointed my way.

Millwood broke our press the next time down the floor, but their half-court offense couldn't convert. Elbows missed a shot, and Mehdi grabbed the rebound.

I brought the ball up and ran our offense. At the top of the key, I passed to Dylan on the right and set a screen for Mehdi. Then I kept moving, cutting down and across the paint.

"Jason!" I waved him my way.

He ran off my shoulder, and then I stood up straight and perfectly still with my feet a little more than shoulder width apart and my arms crossed in front. I braced for impact. Super-Size lowered his shoulder and barreled into me. But I stood my ground. That's not to say he didn't lift me *off* the ground. It felt like a sledgehammer hit my chest, but I slowed him down.

Jason caught Dylan's pass in the paint and turned. He had a clear look. He sank the shot.

Tie game.

That's how things stayed. For the rest of the half, neither team went up by more than two points. Even when the Bench Mob was in the game, and Coach Acevedo kept them in for a while so that the starters would have fresh legs for the finish, the game remained close.

With a little over a minute left, we trailed 29–28. We had the ball and a chance to take the lead.

"I want the shot," I said to my teammates. I patted the front of my jersey. "Get me open. I'll make it."

I got the ball near half-court and blew past Elbows. Fingernails slid over, but I was ready for him. I planted my right foot between his legs, lifted my toes, and heel-pivoted. Then, off balance and out of control, I whip-spun around him.

The same move I did against Cypress Village . . . in reverse!

I wasn't done. I went hard to the rim, right at Mega-Man, and got off the shot. He smacked me on the arm and bumped me with his hip.

The ref called the foul. The ball went in.

"Boss!" I popped my jersey and then high-fived my teammates.

"Rip! Rip! Rip!" the Bench Mob cheered.

As I set myself on the line, I checked the clock. Thirty-seven seconds. We led by one. We had one time-out left. Millwood didn't have any.

"After I make this," I said, looking from Mehdi to Dylan to Jason to Keith, "we press hard. Make them work. They're gassed."

I stepped to the line and calmly sank the free throw.

31–29.

Millwood got the ball inbounds, but we made them work. It took them four passes to get across the timeline.

Twenty-nine seconds.

Super-Size passed to Fingernails in the corner. Fingernails took the shot. It banged off the back of the rim. Under the boards, both teams batted around the ball. Somehow, Fingernails came up with it and dribbled out.

Twenty-two seconds.

"No fouls!" Coach Acevedo shouted. "No fouls!"

I guarded Fingernails tight as he dribbled cross-court. I wasn't going to foul him, but I wasn't about to let him have it easy. He passed to Mega-Man at the elbow, who put up a shot. It hit off the side of the rim and went out of bounds under the basket.

Clifton United ball.

Fourteen seconds left.

Coach Acevedo called our final time-out.

"Here's what we're going to do," he said in our huddle. He motioned for the kids in close to kneel and for the kids in back to move in. "You ready?" He looked around and made eye contact with a bunch of us. He stopped on Red.

I flinched. I knew what was about to happen. It was brilliant. A brilliant coaching move by Coach Acevedo.

"They're going to foul us." Coach Acevedo soccer-style kicked up the ball by his foot and kneed it to Red. "That means it's time for our free-throw-shooting machine. You up for it?"

Red hopped from foot to foot. "I'm playing in the game?"

"You are."

"I'm allowed to play in the game, Coach Acevedo?"

"You are. You have permission."

He spun to me. "Did you hear that, Mason Irving?" His basketball smile took over his face. "I'm in the game."

I hammer-fisted the air and slid next to him. "You got this."

"Oh, yeah, Mason Irving. Clifton United goes thirteen deep. Everyone contributes."

"They're going to hit you hard," I said. "Really hard. It could be Super-Size or Mega-Man."

"Clifton United goes thirteen deep." Red pulled off his Bench Mob shirt. He smoothed out his jersey and brushed his number twenty-four. "Everyone contributes, Mason Irving."

"We're going to beat them again, Red," Coach Acevedo said. "We're going to beat them again."

"We're pushing the envelope." Red's smile couldn't go wider. "Aren't we, Coach Acevedo?"

"We most certainly are." Coach Acevedo gave him a pound. "Let's push it even further." He turned to Max. "You're in, too. You're setting one of the screens for Red. You up for it?"

"Oh, yeah!" Max raised his arm. "If Red's up for it, I'm up for it."

"I'm up for it, Max Stevens."

A moment later, Jason, Keith, Max, Red, and I took the floor. We had our instructions: Set screens. Get the ball to Red.

"Here we go," I play-by-played under my breath. "Fourteen ticks left on the clock, Clifton United leads by two, trying to end Millwood's season once again."

Red was getting open. Even if it meant I had to knock Millwood players over like bowling pins, Red was getting open.

Tweet!

Out of bounds, Keith smacked the basketball.

Red ran for the far corner, I bolted up to Max at the foul line, and Jason slid toward the near corner. I set the screen for Max, and he curled off my shoulder and ran a few steps. Then he planted his feet and folded his arms across his chest. Red brushed Max's shoulder as he sped by. Then he brushed my shoulder and ran off the second screen.

That second screen wasn't needed. Max had already taken out Fingernails. Red was open. Keith passed him the ball. Red caught it, wrapped his arms around the rock, and waited.

Fingernails fouled him a second later, bumping Red from behind. Hard, but not too hard.

Tweet!

I raced over to Red. "You good?"

He stood up slowly. His face was squinched, his arms still wrapped around the ball.

"You got two shots," I said. "Can you—"

"I'm Clifton United's free-throw-shooting machine," he said softly.

"You are, Blake Daniels." I reached over and ruffled his hair. He ducked away, but not before I got in a good shake.

Red's smile returned.

"I need the ball, Number Twenty-Four," the referee stepped to Red.

Red quickly handed it to him and bolted to the line.

"It all comes down to this," I announced. "Red's on the . . ."

I stopped.

Suddenly, everything was gone—the clock, Coach Crazy, the crowd, the Bench Mob, the music, the players, everything. Except for Red and me. We were the only ones in the gym, the silent and still gym.

Red was locked in. I was locked in.

He trapped the ball soccer-style under his left foot, placed a finger over each earplug, and took a few breaths. With both hands, he picked up the ball, squared his shoulders, and looked at the front rim. Then he dribbled three times low to the ground—hard dribbles that echoed and lingered. He stood back up and spun the ball until his fingers were around the word SPALDING. He looked at the rim again, extended his arms, and took the shot.

Underhanded.

Swish.

32–29, eleven seconds.

One more. This was the one that counted. This was the one that would put the game out of reach.

Red was still locked in. I was still locked in.

He went through his routine and shot the free throw.

Underhanded.

Swish!

"Boo-yah!" I hammer-fisted the air.

"Bam!" Red raised his arm.

33–29, eleven seconds.

"No fouls!" Coach Acevedo said. "No fouls!"

We let Millwood get the ball inbounds, but we didn't let them bring it up the floor untouched. By the time Elbows rushed his three-pointer, there were only four seconds left. The ball hit the backboard and landed in my hands. I threw it back into the air. Before it landed, the final horn sounded.

Clifton 33, Millwood 29.

"You did it again!" I raced up to Red.

"We did it, Mason Irving!"

I ruffled his hair, but this time, Red didn't duck or move away. And as everyone raced over, Red basketball-smiled his biggest basketball smile ever.

"Let's circle up!" I called.

All twelve Clifton United huddled at the free-throw line. We draped our arms around one another and swayed from side to side.

"Every little thing we do matters," I said. I chin-nodded at Red and then looked around at my teammates. "Everyone's doing our handshake, with one difference."

I explained, and in less than a nanosecond everyone had paired off. I was with Red.

"Roll left, roll right," Clifton United chanted. "Slap right, slap left."

Everyone jumped, bumped hips, and on the landing . . .

"Zwibble!"

Clifton United
Clifton
Clifton United

Acknowledgments

There are so many I need to acknowledge. Thanks and love to . . .

Wes Adams, my editor. You continue to challenge me. You continue to push me. Keep on keepin' on.

Andrew Arnold, the designer whose vision for this series far exceeds my wildest expectations.

Mary Van Akin, Katie Halata, Lucy Del Priore, and the entire team at Farrar Straus Giroux and the Macmillan Children's Publishing Group. A dream team has rallied behind my series. What more could an author hope for?

Tim Probert, the illustrator whose images bring Rip and Red to life.

Erin Murphy, my agent. You make it happen and get it done. I treasure it all.

Jean Dayton, my booking agent. The best in the business . . . even though you root for the Cubbies.

Anna Rekate, my friend and fellow educator, who reads

through my early drafts and provides the no-nonsense feedback I crave.

Donalyn Miller, your *Reading in the Wild* and *The Book Whisperer* should be required reading for all teachers. Mr. Acevedo's Where I Read mini project was inspired by your words.

Rachel Carr, whom I taught middle school with way back in the day at P.S. 333. When I visited your class at P.S. 130 in Lower Manhattan a few years ago, you introduced me to one of your students, Zachary Maxwell, a blossoming filmmaker who had just completed a short documentary, *Yuck.* That film inspired one of the storylines in this book.

Zachary Maxwell, your film *Yuck* now serves as the answer to a question I'm often asked: Do you ever get ideas from school visits?

Ezra Azrieli Holzman, a superhero kid and friend who introduced me to the word *prestanderous* while guest-hosting the YouTube series *Sez Me.*

Holly Morgan-Winsdale, who told me all about Zwibble and allowed me to use it in this book.

Kareem Eid, who as a teenager traveled with me to New Orleans on a post–Hurricane Katrina volunteer trip, and who, ever since, has taught me so much about growing up and being Muslim in America in the twenty-first century.

Kevin, my husband, my family.

GOFISH

QUESTIONS FOR THE AUTHOR

PHIL BILDNER

What did you want to be when you grew up?
I wanted to be a basketball player or baseball player, but size and ability got in the way. I guess I wanted to be a lawyer because that's what the people in my life told me I wanted to be. Fortunately, I realized I had to be what *I* wanted to be.

When did you realize you wanted to be a writer?
I always loved to write, but I never considered it for a career until I was teaching middle school in the New York City public schools. My students and experiences there inspired me to write.

What's your favorite childhood memory?
Going to ball games! I loved going to Shea Stadium to watch the New York Mets, Nassau Coliseum to watch the New York Islanders, and Madison Square Garden to watch the New York Knicks.

As a young person, who did you look up to most?
I don't know if there was one person in particular that I looked up to. Of course, I had favorite athletes, musicians, and statesmen, but I don't think there was any one individual or hero that I aspired to be like more than anyone else.

What was your favorite thing about school?

In fifth grade, my teacher was Mr. Kramer. He was my first male teacher, and he ran his classroom in an unconventional manner. More than any other teacher, he made school and learning fun.

What were your hobbies as a kid? What are your hobbies now?

As a kid, I loved playing ball and playing with my dogs. I would also spend hours on my bedroom floor playing Strat-O-Matic Baseball, the pre-cursor to fantasy baseball. My hobbies now include reading, hiking, working out, and traveling. I still love playing ball and playing with my dog (obviously, it's a different dog).

Did you play sports as a kid?

I did! I played baseball, basketball, and soccer. I always wanted to be outside running around. No matter where I went, I always looked for a pick-up game of hoops.

What was your first job, and what was your "worst" job?

My first job was shoveling snow. My friend Steven and I would go around and knock on doors every time it snowed. Easy money and all cash! My worst job was when I worked at Wendy's with my friend Mitchell. We lasted two nights. Then we got a job packing bicycles and bicycle parts in a warehouse . . . which really wasn't all that much better.

What book is on your nightstand right now?

Lately, I've been reading young adult novels. I highly recommend three incredibly relevant ones that I know I'll be reading more than once: *The Hate U Give by* Angie Thomas, *American Street* by Ibi Zoboi, and *The Poet X* by Elizabeth Acevedo.

How did you celebrate publishing your first book?
My first book was *Shoeless Joe & Black Betsy.* We had a publication party at Books of Wonder, a bookstore in New York City. At the time, I was still teaching middle school. Many of my students and their families attended. It was pretty special.

Where do you write your books?
All different places! I take a writer's notebook with me wherever I go. When I lived in the city, I would write on the subway all the time. I also enjoyed writing on the roof of my apartment building. Nowadays, most of my writing takes place either in my office at home or on my back porch. When I'm on the road, you'll find me writing on airplanes and in my hotel room. I guess I can write pretty much anywhere!

What sparked your imagination for the Rip and Red series?
When I visit schools, I always tell kids to write about what you know and love. I taught middle school for many years. I played basketball for many years. Nowadays, I visit schools around the world and interact with kids and educators in ways I never imagined. My life experiences—past and current—inspired me to write this series.

What challenges do you face in the writing process, and how do you overcome them?
I don't have enough time to write all the things I want to write. It forces me to prioritize. For instance, as I'm answering these questions, I'm finishing up the third Rip and Red book.

However, I've already got my eye on a picture book manuscript I worked on a couple of years ago that wasn't clicking, but now I think I found the way to make it sing. I can't wait to dive back in. I also can't wait to work on an idea for an early chapter book. I need to clone myself!

What is your favorite word?
Empathy.

If you could live in any fictional world, what would it be?
The Hogwarts School of Witchcraft and Wizardry. Because it is the Hogwarts School of Witchcraft and Wizardry.

Who is your favorite fictional character?
Ignatius Reilly from John Kennedy Toole's *A Confederacy of Dunces.*

What was your favorite book when you were a kid? Do you have a favorite book now?
As a kid, I read the newspaper every morning. I would sit in the middle of the kitchen floor and devour the sports pages of *The New York Times*. I also read lots of sports biographies. Then in sixth grade, I read a book I wasn't allowed to read because it was supposedly too grown up for me. I read *Alive* by Piers Paul Read, the story of the rugby team whose plane crashed in the Andes Mountains. It was intense! My favorite book now? That's easy. All the ones I read aloud to my students are my all-time faves. Those were the best reading moments of my life.

If you could travel in time, where would you go and what would you do?
I would travel back in time and visit my teenage self and tell him to have the courage and conviction to be the person he really is.

What's the best advice you have ever received about writing?

Read. In order to write, you have to read. It doesn't matter what you're reading, so long as you're reading something.

What advice do you wish someone had given you when you were younger?

Live your life, not the life others want you to live or the life you think you're supposed to live.

Do you ever get writer's block? What do you do to get back on track?

I rarely get writer's block, but if I ever need to jump-start my writing, I usually find a different place to write. A change of scenery—more often than not—does the trick.

What do you want readers to remember about your books?

That they were able to see themselves or an aspect of themselves in the books, and as a result, they're books they want to share with others.

What would you do if you ever stopped writing?

I hope I never have to find out the real answer to that question, but if I wasn't writing, I'd be teaching in some capacity.

If you were a superhero, what would your superpower be?

Over the years, I've answered this question in many different ways. I've wanted to be able to turn invisible, time travel, shape-shift, and fly (among many others). Right now, I'm thinking I'd want a pause button—the power to stop everything so that I can do all the things I want and need to do, and also to arrange things in the way that I want them to be.

Do you have any strange or funny habits? Did you when you were a kid?

I'll tell you about one I have now: When I lived in the city, I would sometimes go up to the rooftop of my apartment building, plug in my music, and dance like nobody's watching . . . only I know there had to be lots of people watching from other buildings and windows. I'm sure some stranger shot some vid of me doing this and posted it on YouTube. Now I do the dancing-by-myself thing in my backyard.

What do you consider to be your greatest accomplishment?

That's a tough one, but I'll go with a sports one. I ran the New York City Marathon twice. The first time I ran it, I barely even trained. At the time, I wasn't even a runner. I just played basketball and worked out. My friend had an extra number, so I ran with him. When I finished, I was tired, but I actually had a little gas left in the tank. So the next year, I trained and set an ambitious goal. I told myself if met my goal, I'd never run another marathon. I did it!

What would your readers be most surprised to learn about?

Whenever I visit schools, if kids haven't seen a picture of me or visited my website and watched my vids, they're always surprised by my appearance. They don't think I look like a writer . . . whatever a writer is supposed to look like!

It's spring of their fifth-grade year, and Rip and Red have a thrilling opportunity to play in a weekend tournament of champions. But it will mean facing new challenges, leaving their comfort zone, and learning the true meaning of the word *champion*.

Keep reading for an excerpt.

One-on-One-on-One

"Next basket wins," I said, clapping for the ball.

"No," Diego said. "Win by two."

"Win by two, Mason Irving," Red said as he spun around the pole under the basket.

Diego, Red, and I were the only three in the Reese Jones Elementary schoolyard. All the other kids were waiting at the car pickup line or getting on the buses to go home.

"Yo, it's always win by two at RJE," Diego said.

"How do you know?" I said. "You never play."

I'd never seen Diego play hoops before, which is why I had no idea he could ball. Seriously ball.

"Ten for Diego Vasquez, ten for Mason Irving." Red pointed at me. "It's always win by two at RJE."

"Whose friend are you?" I said.

"Both!" Red let go of the pole and hopped from foot to foot.

Red's my best friend. He calls everyone by their first and

last name. To him, I'm Mason Irving. To everyone else, I'm Rip. It's a basketball nickname.

I placed the ball on my hip and shook out my dreadlocks.

Diego shook out his hair, too.

"Here's the scene," Diego said, smiling. "You're lying on your bed, and rhino dung is dripping from the ceiling. It's all over you. It's on your face. It's even in your mouth."

All game long, Diego had been talking trash, mocking me, and saying nasty stuff.

I cut right, got a half-step on him, and took a shot from inside the elbow. It clanked off the back of the rim.

"You tried, son." Diego grabbed the rebound and dribbled to the top of the key. He gestured with his chin at Red. "Time for me to finish off your little friend."

"I'm taller than you are," I said.

I lunged for the ball, but Diego blocked my hand with his shoulder. He then spun past me and drove in for a layup.

"Boom! In your face!" he shouted.

"Eleven for Diego Vasquez, ten for Mason Irving," Red announced.

Diego toe-flipped the ball off the cement and jogged to the top of the key. "You're going down, son," he said.

"We'll see."

"It's next basket now." He shook out his hair again. "Check." He passed me the ball.

24

I punched it back.

Diego swung the ball back and forth by his shins. He wanted to go left—Diego was a lefty—so I gave him the right.

He drove left, but instead of going lower-the-shoulder hard like he had been all game, he backed me down. A couple steps from the hoop, he put up a shot.

It bounced off the front rim. I boxed him out for the rebound.

"Who's your daddy?" I said, dribbling out.

"Go, Mason Irving!" Red shouted.

"Time for me to stick a fork in your butt," I said. "You're done, *son*."

Diego wasn't the only one chirping. I'd been dishing out the trash talk as much as he had.

"It's Irving's turn," I play-by-played. I love doing play-by-play. "Vasquez had a chance to put this one away, but he left the door open. Irving slides right and sizes up the court. He dribbles baseline . . . He shoots . . ."

"No good!" Diego bodied me for the board. "Now it's Vasquez's turn," he said, mocking my announcing. "Watch him stick a fork in Irving's butt and show him who's really done."

Diego lowered his shoulder and drove left. He put up a shot and banked it in.

"Ballgame!" He pounded his chest and stomped across the paint. "Who's your daddy now?"

Red laughed along. "Who's your daddy now?"

Diego stepped to Red. "What are you laughing at?" he said. "Now it's time for me to dispose of *you*."

"Me?" Red pointed to himself.

"Yeah, you." Diego gripped the pole under the basket and spun around. "Time for me to beat you at free throws."

"Ha!" I said. "This I'd like to see."

Red's a free-throw-shooting beast. I've seen him hit twenty and thirty in a row tons of times. When Red's locked in at the line, he's money.

"First one to miss loses," Diego said, backpedaling to the line.

"Make him shoot underhanded," I said to Red.

"Oh, yeah." Red shook his fists by his shoulders. "You have to shoot underhanded, Diego Vasquez."

That's how Red shoots his free throws. He goes through this whole routine and then shoots the ball underhanded.

"Underhand, overhand, behind the back, whatever." Diego bobbed his head.

I tossed him the ball. "No pressure."

Diego glanced at Red and then placed his toes on the line. He power-dribbled a few times and spun the ball in his hands like Red does before he takes his foul shots.

"No pressure," I said again.

Diego shot the underhanded free throw. It banged off the backboard without hitting the rim.

"Ha!" I laughed. I pounded my chest and stomped across the lane like Diego had a minute ago. "Ballgame!"

"Yo, Red still has to make his," Diego said.

"Put him away," I said to Red, and then spun back to Diego. "Watch how it's done, *son*."

Red set himself on the line and trapped the ball under his left foot soccer-style. He took several breaths, picked up the ball, and squared his shoulders.

"I could say some wack things right now," Diego said, leaning in. "You want to hear some wack things?"

It didn't matter what Diego said. Red wasn't hearing any of it. He was locked in.

Red dribbled three times low and hard and stood back up. Then he spun the ball until his fingers were right and looked at the rim. He extended his arms and took the shot.

Underhanded.

Swish!

"Boo-yah!" I hammer-fisted the air.

"Bam!" Red cheered. He smiled his super-wide basketball smile. "Who's your daddy now, Diego Vasquez?"

Road Trip

"The free-throw-shooting machine strikes again!" someone said.

We all turned.

Our teacher, Mr. Acevedo, was jogging onto the court.

"Well done." He gave Red a pound.

"Thanks, Mr. Acevedo."

Mr. Acevedo's the coolest and best teacher we've ever had. All the fifth graders think so.

Mr. Acevedo had asked Diego, Red, and me to wait for him until after Thunder Dome. That's what he calls the car pickup line during dismissal. Mr. Acevedo has Thunder Dome duty every afternoon.

We walked over to the Amp, the amphitheater at the far end of the playground. The Amp's where Mr. Acevedo sometimes holds Teacher's Theater Time. That's when he reads to the class. Mr. Acevedo tries to read to the class every day. Right now, he's reading us *The Fourteenth Goldfish.*

"Let's get right down to business," he said. He sat on the front bench and faced the three of us. "So I spoke to all your—"

"Wait for me!"

We all turned again.

A girl was running toward us.

"It's Maya Wade!" Red waved his arms like a football referee at the end of a play. "Maya Wade's here."

Maya played with us on our basketball team, Clifton United, but because she didn't go to RJE, I hadn't seen her since the season ended back in the fall. I couldn't believe how tall she was. We used to be the same size, but now she had five or six inches on me, like almost all the other fifth-grade girls.

"Hey, boys." She straddled the seat next to Mr. Acevedo. "Did I miss anything?"

"Not at all," he said. "Perfect timing."

"Long time no see," Diego said to her.

She smiled. "Very."

I checked Diego. I didn't know he and Maya knew each other.

"How was school?" Mr. Acevedo asked Maya.

"The same," she answered. "I brought Carolina to Makerspace." Carolina was Maya's little sister. "Someone will drop her at the house afterward."

"I'll let Aisha know."

Aisha was Mr. Acevedo's girlfriend. Sometimes she met Mr. Acevedo at school. I didn't know they knew Maya outside of basketball.

"I asked Maya to join us," Mr. Acevedo said. He strummed his legs. "Let's get back down to business. So I spoke to all your moms."

"That's never a good sign," I said.

"For the record," Diego said, holding up his hands, "I had nothing to do with sticking the juice box straws up the first graders' noses. Not this time."

"I'll make a note of it," Mr. Acevedo said. "Relax, Diego. No one here's in any trouble."

To be perfectly honest, when Mr. Acevedo said he spoke to all our moms, I did get a little tingly, because I didn't exactly have a squeaky-clean record this year. Back in the fall, I got into this thing with Avery Goodman, this girl in my class who uses a wheelchair and sometimes gets an attitude (but now we're friends). Then a bunch of us—including Diego, Red, and Avery—got in trouble for Operation Food Fight (which was actually pretty cool and creative). Then I got into this other thing with Tiki Eid, the new girl on the basketball team (but she's no longer here).

"Clifton United is taking a road trip," Mr. Acevedo said. Mr. Acevedo is also coach of our Clifton United basketball team. "We've been invited to play in a tournament of champions."

"Ballin'!" Maya banged her hands like cymbals.

"Outstanding!" I said.

"Oh, yeah!" Red said. "Outstanding."

"So why am I here?" Diego rested his arm on my shoulder. "I'm not on Clifton United."

"Well, Diego, that's what I spoke to your mom *and* uncle about," Mr. Acevedo said. "They both said you could join the team."

"Don't play, Mr. Acevedo," Diego said.

"I'm not playing."

"I'm not well, you know."

"Actually, you are well, Diego." Mr. Acevedo tucked his hair behind his ears. "That's why you can play, if you want to."

"I want to, I want to, I want to!" Diego pounded the bench with both fists. "Yes, yes, yes!" He jumped up and danced in circles on the bench. "It's about time they let me off my leash!"

For a while, Diego was sick, really sick. He missed the whole second half of third grade and the beginning of fourth. When he came back to school, he always wore hats, goofy ones with earflaps and tie strings, because his medicines made his hair fall out.

"I got to shoot around with Diego over the weekend," Mr. Acevedo said to me. "So did Maya. We ran into his family at the park. I had no idea he could ball."

“Neither did Rip,” Diego said, pretending to tomahawk-dunk on me. He sat back down. “I schooled him!”

I ruffled Diego’s hair. Red ruffled his hair, too.

Diego had hair now. Even though he stopped wearing his hats a few months ago, I’m still not used to seeing him without them. Every time I look his way, I expect to see a black-and-white dog with huge brown eyes peering into my soul or a one-eyed blue-and-yellow Minion staring a hole into my brain.

“Yes, yes, yes!” Diego pounded the bench again. “I can’t

believe my uncle's down with this. He never lets me do anything."

"Both your mom and your uncle are on board," Mr. Acevedo said.

"But how am I allowed to play?" Diego asked. "I wasn't on the team in the fall."

"We got you a health waiver," Mr. Acevedo said.

"Sweet," Diego said.

My basketball brain started to churn. I couldn't wait to play in the same backcourt as Diego. I loved playing with lefties, especially lefties who knew what to do. Diego was also nonstop movement. Just like me. If Diego had been on Clifton United during fall ball, we wouldn't have just made the playoffs, we would've won the whole thing.

"Let me tell you about the tournament," Mr. Acevedo said. He crossed his legs and grabbed his ankles. "It's called the Jack Twyman Spring Showdown, and it takes place at the Hoops Haven Sports Complex. Sixteen teams have been invited. It's two rounds of pool play followed by a single-elimination knockout stage. Every team plays a minimum of three games."

"This is going to be sick," Diego said, bobbing his head.

"Who else is on the team?" Maya asked.

"From fall ball, it's the four of you, plus Mehdi Karmoune. The rest of the roster is kids from teams we played against."

"Are they trying out?" I said.

"Not enough time." Mr. Acevedo shook his head. "The Showdown's Easter weekend. Less than two weeks from now." He tapped my knee. "We're counting on you big-time, Rip. We need you to pick up where you left off at the end of fall ball. You're Clifton United's floor leader, our team general. I'm going to be pushing you hard, real hard."

"Bring it," I said.

DON'T MISS THE OTHER ADVENTURES OF RIP AND RED!

"Pure fun with a lot of heart."

—*School Library Journal* on *A Whole New Ballgame*